The Folk of the Faraway Tree

Jo, Bessie and Fanny have been looking forward to cousin Connie's visit, but she turns out to be awfully spoilt and stuck-up. She won't believe a word when the children tell her all about the magic tree in the forest, but soon she has to change her mind, and the tree's many marvels help her to become a much nicer little girl.

Enid Blyton needs no introduction to her readers. Author of around 400 books, which have been translated into almost every language, she has been known and loved by children of all ages for many years.

Other Enid Blyton stories available in Beavers include *The Magic Faraway Tree*, *The Wishing-Chair Again* and *The Enchanted Wood*.

Other Enid Blyton titles
available in
Beaver

The Folk of the Faraway Tree

Enid Blyton

Illustrated by Lesley Smith

Beaver Books

Revised edition published in 1972 by Dean & Son Limited
52–54 Southwark Street, London SE1 1VA

This paperback edition published in 1978 by
The Hamlyn Publishing Group Limited
London · New York · Sydney · Toronto
Astronaut House, Feltham, Middlesex, England
Tenth impression 1982

© Copyright Text Darrell Waters Limited 1946
© Copyright Illustrations
The Hamlyn Publishing Group Limited 1978
ISBN 0 600 33663 8

Reproduced, printed and bound in Great Britain by
Cox & Wyman Limited, Reading

Contents

I.

Curious Connie Comes to Stay

One day Mother came to the three children, as they worked out in the garden, and spoke to them.

"Jo! Bessie! Fanny! Listen to me for a minute. I've just had a letter from an old friend of mine, and I am wondering what to do about it. I'll read it to you."

Mother read the letter:

"DEAR OLD FRIEND,

"Please will you do something for me? I have not been well for some time, and the doctor says I must go away on a long holiday. But, as you know, I have a little girl, Connie, and I cannot leave her by herself. So would you please let her stay with you until I come back? I will, of course, pay you well. Your three children are good and well-behaved, and I feel that their friendship will be very nice for my little Connie, who is, I am afraid, rather spoilt. Do let me know soon.

"Your old friend,

"LIZZIE HAYNES."

The three children listened in silence. Then Bessie spoke.

"Oh Mother! We've seen Connie once, and she was awfully stuck-up and spoilt—and awfully curious too, sticking her nose into everything!

Have we *got* to have her?"

"No, of course not," said Mother. "But I could do with some extra money, you know—and I do think that Connie might soon settle down and stop being spoilt if she lived with us. It would be good for her!"

"And I suppose we ought to help people if we can," said Jo. "All right, Mother—we'll have Connie, shall we, and just teach her not to be spoilt!"

"We shall be able to show her the Enchanted Wood and the Faraway Tree!" said Fanny.

"Yes—we used to have Cousin Dick, but now he's gone back home," said Bessie. "We'll have Connie instead! If you put a little bed into the corner of my room and Fanny's, Mother, we can have her in there."

Mother smiled at them and went indoors to write to her old friend, to say yes, she would have Connie. The children looked at one another.

"We'll soon tick Connie off if she starts any of her high-and-mighty ways here," said Bessie.

"And we'll stop her poking her nose into everything too!" said Fanny. "I say—what about taking her up the Faraway Tree and letting her peep in at the Angry Pixie? He'll soon tick her off!"

The others giggled. They could see that they would have a bit of fun with Connie. She was always so curious and inquisitive about everything and everyone. Well—she would get a few shocks in the Enchanted Wood!

"It will be fun showing somebody else the Faraway Tree, and all the people there," said Jo. "I wonder what Curious Connie will think of the Saucepan Man, and Silky and Moon-Face!"

"And I wonder what they will think of *her!*" said Bessie. "What a lovely name for her, Jo—Curious Connie! I shall always think of her like that now!"

Curious Connie was to come the next week. Bessie helped Mother put a little bed into the corner of the girls' bedroom. Connie wasn't very big. She was as old as Fanny, but she had been very fussy over her food, and so she hadn't grown as well as she ought to. She was a pretty, dainty little thing, fond of nice clothes and ribbons.

"Brush that untidy hair, Fanny, before you meet Connie," said Mother. Fanny's hair had grown rather long, and needed a trim.

The children went to meet the 'bus. "There it is!" cried Jo. "Coming round the corner. And there's Curious Connie on it, look—all dressed up as if she was going to a party!"

Connie jumped off the 'bus, carrying a bag. Jo politely took it from her, and gave her a welcoming kiss. The girls welcomed her too. Connie looked them up and down.

"My, you do look country folk!" she said.

"Well, that's what we are," said Bessie. "You'll look like us soon, too. I hope you'll be very happy here, Connie."

"I saw Dick the other day," said Connie, as she walked demurely along the lane with the others.

"He told me the most awful stories!"

"*Dick* did! But he's not a story-teller!" said Jo, in surprise. "What sort of stories did he tell you?"

"Well, he told me about a silly Enchanted Wood and a ridiculous Faraway Tree, and some stupid people called Moon-Face and Dame Washalot and Mister Watzisname, and a mad fellow called the Saucepan Man who was deaf," said Connie.

"Oh! Do you think all those were silly and stupid?" said Jo at last.

"I didn't believe in any of it," said Connie. "I don't believe in things like that — fairies or brownies or magic or anything. It's old-fashioned."

"Well, we must be *jolly* old-fashioned then," said Bessie. "Because we not only believe in the Enchanted Wood and the Faraway Tree and love our funny friends there, but we go to see them too — and we visit the lands at the top of the Tree as well! We did think of taking you too!"

"It wouldn't be much use," said Connie. "I shouldn't believe in them at all."

"What — not even if you saw them?" cried Fanny.

"I don't think so," said Connie. "I mean — it all sounds quite impossible to me. Really it does."

"Well, we'll see," said Jo. "It looks as if we'll have some fun with you, up the Faraway Tree, Connie! I should just like to see the Angry Pixie's face if you tell him you don't believe in him!"

"Let's take her to-morrow!" said Bessie, with a giggle.

"All right!" said Jo. "But we'd better not let her go into any Land at the top of the Tree. She'd never get down again!"

"What Land? At the top of the *Tree*? A land at the top of a tree!" said Connie, puzzled.

"Yes," said Bessie. "You see, the Enchanted Wood is quite near here, Connie. And in the middle of it is the biggest, tallest tree in the world—very magic indeed. It's called the Faraway Tree, because its top is so far away, and always sticks up into some queer magic land there—a different one every week."

"I don't believe a word of it," said Connie.

"All right. Don't, then," said Fanny, beginning

to feel cross. "Look—here we are, home—and there's Mother looking out for us!"

Soon Connie and the girls were unpacking Connie's bag and putting her things away into two empty drawers in the chest. Bessie saw that there were no really sensible country clothes at all. However could Connie climb the Faraway Tree in a dainty frock? She ought to have some old clothes! Well, she and Fanny had plenty so they could lend her some.

"I suppose you are longing to show Connie the Enchanted Wood!" said Mother, when they went down to tea.

"Oh—do *you* believe in it too?" said Connie, surprised that a grown-up should do so.

"Well, I haven't seen the Tree, but I have seen some of the people that come down it," said Mother.

"Look—here's one of them now!" said Jo, jumping up as he saw someone coming in at the front gate. It was Moon-Face, his round face beaming happily. He carried a note in his hand.

"Hallo!" said Jo, opening the door. "Come in and have some tea, Moon-Face. We've got a little friend here—the girl I was telling you about—Connie."

"Ah—how do you do?" said Moon-Face, going all polite as he saw the dainty, pretty Connie. "I've come to ask you to tea with me and Silky to-morrow, Connie. I hope you can come. Any friend of the children's is welcome up the Faraway Tree!"

Connie shook hands with the queer, round-faced little man. She hardly knew what to say. If she said she would go to tea with him she was as good as saying that she believed in all this nonsense about the Faraway Tree—and she certainly didn't!

"Moon-Face, you have put poor Connie into a fix," said Jo, grinning. "She doesn't believe in you, you see—so how can she come to tea with a person she doesn't believe in, at a place she thinks isn't there?"

"Quite easily," said Moon-Face. "Let her think it is a dream. Let her think *I'm* a dream."

"All right," said Connie, who really was longing to go to tea with Moon-Face, but felt she couldn't believe in him, after all she had said. "All right. I'll come. I'll think you're just a dream. You probably are, anyway."

"And I'll think *you* are a dream too," said Moon-Face, politely. "Then it will be nice for both of us."

"Well, I'm not a dream!" said Connie, rather indignantly. "I should have thought you could see quite well I'm real, and not a dream."

Moon-Face grinned. "I hope you're a good dream, and not a bad one, if you *are* a dream," he said. "Well—see you all to-morrow. Four o'clock, in my house at the top of the tree. Will you walk up, or shall I send down cushions on a rope for you?"

"We'll walk up," said Jo. "We rather want Connie to meet the people who live in the Tree.

She won't believe in any of them, but they'll believe in her all right—and it might be rather funny!"

"It certainly will!" said Moon-Face, and went off, grinning again, leaving Silky's polite invitation note in Connie's small hand.

"I'm not sure I like him very much," said Connie, taking the last bun off the plate.

"What—not like *Moon-Face*!" cried Fanny, who really loved the queer little man. "He's the dearest, darlingest, kindest, funniest, nicest——"

"All right, all right," said Connie. "Don't go on for hours like that. I'll go to-morrow—but I still say it's all make-believe and pretence, and not really real!"

"You wait and see!" said Jo. "Come on—we've time for a game before bed . . . and to-morrow, Connie, to-morrow, you shall go up the Faraway Tree!"

2.

Up the Faraway Tree

The next day was bright and sunny. Connie woke up feeling rather excited. She was away from home, staying in the country—she had three play-mates instead of being an only child—and they had promised to take her up the Faraway Tree!

"Even if I don't believe in it, it will be fun to see what they think it is," she said to herself.

"I hope we have a good time, and a nice tea."

The children usually had to do some kind of work in the mornings, even though it was holidays. The girls had to help their mother, and Jo had to work in the garden. There was a good deal to do there, for there had been some rain, and the weeds had come up by the hundred.

Connie didn't very much like having to help to make the beds, but the children's mother was quite firm with her.

"You will do just the same as the others," she said. "And don't pout like that, Connie. I don't like it. It makes you look really ugly."

Connie was not used to being spoken to like this. Her mother had always fussed round her and spoilt her, and she had been the one and only child in the house. Now she was one of four, and things were very different.

"Cheer up!" said Bessie, seeing tears in Connie's eyes. "Don't be a spoilt baby! Think of our treat this afternoon!"

Connie sniffed. "Funny sort of treat!" she said, but all the same she did cheer up.

When three o'clock came Mother said the children might go. "It will take you some time to get up the Tree, I am sure, if you are going to show Connie everything," she said. "And please don't let her get wet with Dame Washalot's water, will you?"

Connie looked up in astonishment. "Dame Washalot's water!" she said. "Whatever do you mean?"

Bessie giggled. "There's an old woman who lives up the Tree, who is always washing," she said. "She simply adores washing, and when she has finished she tips up her wash-tub, and the soapy water comes sloshing down the tree. You have to look out for it."

"I don't believe a word of it!" said Connie, and she didn't. "Doing washing up a tree! It sounds quite mad to me."

"Let's go now," said Bessie, "or we shan't be at Moon-Face's by four o'clock."

"I must go and change into a pretty frock," said Connie.

"No, don't," said Fanny. "Go as you are. We don't change into decent clothes when we go up the Tree."

"What—go out to tea in ordinary clothes!" cried Connie. "I just couldn't!" And off she went to put on a dainty white frock.

They all went to the edge of the wood. There was a ditch there. "Jump over this—and you're in the Enchanted Wood!" said Bessie.

They all jumped, Connie too. As soon as she was across the ditch, and heard the trees whispering "wisha, wisha, wisha," as they always did in the Enchanted Wood, Connie felt different. She felt excited and wondering and happy. She felt as if there was magic about—although she didn't believe in magic! It was a simply lovely feeling.

They went through the wood, and came to an enormous tree, with a tremendously thick and knotted trunk. Connie gazed up into the branches.

"Goodness!" she said. "I've never seen such a tree in my life! Is this the Enchanted Tree? How marvellous!"

"Yes," said Jo, enjoying Connie's surprise. "And at the top, as we told you, there is a different land every week. I don't know what land there is now. We don't always go. Sometimes the Lands aren't very nice. Once there was the Land of Bad Temper. That was horrid. And a little while ago there was the Land of Smacks. We didn't go there, you can guess! We asked our friends Silky and Moon-Face what it was like, and they said they didn't know either, but they could hear slaps and smacks going on like pistol-shots all the time!"

"Gracious!" said Connie, alarmed. "I wouldn't like to go to a Land like that. Although, of course," she added quickly, "I don't believe in such a thing."

"Of course you don't," said Jo, with a grin. "You don't believe in the Faraway Tree either, do you?—and yet you are going to climb it. Come on—up we go!"

They swung themselves up on the lower branches. It was a very easy tree to climb. The branches were broad and strong, and so many little folk walked up and down the Tree all day long that little paths had been worn on the broad boughs.

"What sort of a tree is it?" said Connie. "It looks like a cherry-tree to me. Oh look!—there are some ripe cherries—just out of my reach, though. Never mind, I'll pick some farther up."

"Better pick them now, or you may find the tree is growing walnuts a bit higher up," said Bessie, laughing. "It's a magic tree, you know. It grows all kinds of different things at any time!"

Sure enough, when Connie looked for ripe cherries a little way up, she found, to her surprise, that the Tree was now growing horse-chestnut leaves and had prickly cases of conkers! She was surprised and disappointed—and very puzzled. Could it really be a magic tree, then?

Soon they met all kinds of little folk coming down the tree. There were brownies and pixies, a goblin or two, a few rabbits and one or two squirrels. It was odd to see a rabbit up a tree. Connie blinked her eyes to see if she really was looking at rabbits up a tree, but there was no doubt about it; she was. The funny thing was, they were dressed in clothes, too. That was odder than ever.

"Do people live in this Tree?" asked Connie, in astonishment, as they came to a little window let in the big trunk.

"Oh yes—lots of them," said Jo. "But don't go peeping into that window, now, Connie. The Angry Pixie lives inside the little house there, and he does hate people to peep."

"All right, I won't peep," said Connie, who was very curious indeed to know what the little house looked like. She meant to peep, of course. She was far too inquisitive a little girl not to do a bit of prying, if she had the chance!

"My shoe-lace has come undone," she called to the others. "You go on ahead. I'll follow."

"I bet she wants to peep," whispered Jo to Bessie, with a grin. "Come on! Let her!"

They went on to a higher branch. Connie pretended to fiddle about with her shoe, and then, when she saw that the others were a little way up, she climbed quickly over to the little window.

She peeped inside. Oh, what fun! Oh, how lovely! There was a proper little room inside the tree, with a bed and a chair and a table. Sitting writing at the table was the Angry Pixie, his glasses on his nose. He had an enormous ink-pot of ink, and a very small pen, and his fingers were stained with the purple ink.

Connie's shadow at the window made him look up. He saw the little girl there, peeping, and he flew into one of his rages. He shot to his feet, picked up the enormous ink-pot and rushed to his window. He opened it and yelled loudly:

"Peeping again! Everybody peeps in at my window, everybody! I won't have it! I really won't have it."

He emptied the ink-pot all over the alarmed Connie. The ink fell in big spots on her frock, and on her cheek and hands. She was in a terrible mess.

"Oh! Oh! You wicked fellow!" she cried. "Look what you've done to me."

"Well, you shouldn't peep," cried the Angry Pixie, still in a rage. "Now I can't finish my letter. I've no more ink! You bad girl! You horrid peeper!"

"Jo! Bessie! Come and help me!" sobbed

Connie, crying tears of rage and grief down her ink-smudged cheeks.

The Angry Pixie suddenly looked surprised and a little ashamed. "Oh—are you a friend of Jo's?" he asked. "Why didn't you say so? I would have shouted at you for peeping, but I wouldn't have thrown ink at you. Really I wouldn't. Jo should have warned you not to peep."

"I did," said Jo, appearing at the window, too. "It's her own fault. My, you do look a mess, Connie. Come on! We shall never be at Moon-Face's by four o'clock."

Wiping away her tears, Connie followed the others up the tree. They came to another window, and this time the three children looked in—but Connie wouldn't. "No, thank you," she said; "I'm not going to have things thrown at me again. I think the people who live here are horrid."

"You needn't be afraid of peeping in at *this* window," said Jo. "The owl lives here and he always sleeps in the day-time, so he never sees people peeping in. He's a great friend of Silky the pixie. Do look at him lying asleep on his bed. That red night-cap he's got on was knitted for him by Silky. Doesn't he look nice in it?"

But Connie wouldn't look in. She was angry and sulky. She went on up the tree by herself. Jo suddenly heard a sound he knew very well, and he yelled loudly to Connie:

"Hi, Connie, Connie, look out! I can hear Dame Washalot's water coming down the tree. LOOK OUT!"

Connie was just about to answer that she didn't believe in Dame Washalot, *or* her silly water, when a perfect cascade of dirty, soapy water came splashing down the Faraway Tree! It fell all over poor Connie, and soaked her from head to foot! Some of the suds stayed in her hair, and she looked a dreadful sight.

The others had all ducked under broad boughs as soon as they heard the water coming, and they hadn't even a drop on them. Jo began to laugh when he saw Connie. The little girl burst into tears again.

"Let me go home, let me go home!" she wept. "I hate your Faraway Tree. I hate all the people in it! Let me go home!"

A silvery voice called down the Tree. "Who is in trouble? Come up and I'll help you!"

"It's dear little Silky!" said Bessie. "Come on, Connie. She'll get you dry again!"

3.

Connie Meets a Few People

"I don't want to see any more of the horrid people who live in this tree," wept poor Connie. But Jo took her firmly by the elbow and pushed her up a broad bough to where a yellow door stood open in the tree.

In the doorway stood the prettiest little elf it

was possible to see. She had hair that stood out round her head like a golden mist, as fine as silk. She held out her hand to Connie.

"Poor child! Did you get caught in Dame Washalot's water! She has been washing such a lot to-day, and the water has been coming down all day long! Let me dry you."

Connie couldn't help liking this pretty little elf. How dainty she was in her shining frock, and what tiny feet and hands she had!

Silky drew her into her tidy little house. She took a towel from a peg and began to dry Connie. The others told her who she was.

"Yes, I know," said Silky. "We're going up to Moon-Face's house to tea. He said he would ask Mister Watzisname too, but I don't expect he'll come, because I heard him snoring in his deck-chair as usual a little while ago."

"Mister Who?" asked Connie.

"Mister Watzisname," said Silky. "He doesn't know his name nor does anyone else, so we call him Watzisname. We've tried and tried to find out what his name is, but I don't expect we shall ever know now. Unless the Land of Know-All comes — then we might go up there and find out. You can find out anything in the Land of Know-All."

"Oh!" said Jo, thinking of a whole lot of things he would dearly love to know. "We'll go there if it comes."

There suddenly came a curious noise down the tree — a noise of clanking and jingling, crashing and banging. Connie looked alarmed. Whatever would happen next? It sounded as if a hundred saucepans, a few dozen kettles, and some odds and ends of dishes and pans were all falling down the tree together!

Then a voice came floating down the tree, and the children grinned.

"Two books for a book-worm,
Two butts for a goat,
Two winks for a winkle
Who can't sing a note!"

"What a very silly song!" said Connie.

"Yes, isn't it?" said Jo. "It's the kind the old Saucepan Man always sings. It's his 'Two' song. Every line but the last begins with the word 'Two' Anyone can make up a song like that."

"Well, I'm sure I don't want to," said Connie, thinking that everyone in the Faraway Tree must be a little bit mad. "Who's the Saucepan Man? And what's that awful crashing noise?"

"Only his saucepans and kettles and things," said Bessie. "He carries them round with him. He's a darling. Once we saw him without his saucepans and things round him, and we didn't know him. He looked funny—quite different."

A most extraordinary person now came into Silky's tiny house, almost getting stuck in the door. He was covered from head to foot with saucepans, kettles and pans, which were tied round him with string. They jangled and crashed together, so everyone always knew when the Saucepan Man was coming.

Connie stared at him in the greatest surprise. His hat was a very big saucepan, so big that it hid most of his face. Connie could see a wide grin, but that was about all.

"Who's this funny creature?" said Connie, in a loud and rather rude voice.

Now the Saucepan Man was deaf, and he didn't usually hear what was said—but this time he did, and he didn't like it. He tilted back his saucepan hat and stared at Connie.

"Who's this dirty little girl?" he said, in a voice just as loud as Connie's. Connie went red. She glared at the Saucepan Man.

"This is Connie," said Jo. He turned to Connie. "This is Saucepan, a great friend of ours," he said. "We've had lots of adventures together."

"Why is she so dirty?" asked Saucepan, looking at Connie's ink-stained dress and dirty face. "Is she always like that? Why don't you clean her?"

Connie was furious. She was always so clean and dainty and well-dressed—how dare this horrid clanking little man talk about her like that!

"Go away!" she said, angrily.

"Yes, it's a very nice day," said the Saucepan Man, politely, going suddenly deaf.

"Don't stay here and STARE!" shouted Connie.

"I certainly should wash your hair," said the Saucepan Man at once. "It's full of soap-suds."

"I said, 'Don't STARE!'" cried Connie.

"Mind that stair?" said the Saucepan Man, looking round. "Can't see any. Didn't know there were any stairs in the Faraway Tree."

Connie stared at him in rage. "Is he mad?" she said to Jo.

Jo and the others were laughing at this queer conversation. Jo shook his head. "No, Saucepan isn't mad. He's just deaf. His saucepans make such a clanking all the time that the noise gets into his ears, and he can't hear properly. So he keeps making mistakes."

"That's right," said the Saucepan Man, entering into the conversation suddenly. "Cakes. Plenty of them. Waiting for us at Moon-Face's."

"I said 'Mis-*takes*'," said Jo. "Not cakes."

"But Moon-Face's cakes aren't mistakes," said Saucepan, earnestly.

Jo gave it up. "We'd better go up to Moon-Face's," he said. "It's past four o'clock."

"I hope that awful Saucepan Man isn't coming with us," said Connie. For a wonder Saucepan heard what she said. He looked angry.

"I hope this nasty little girl isn't coming with us," he said, in his turn, and glared at Connie.

"Now, now, now," said Silky, and patted the Saucepan Man on one of his kettles. "Don't get cross. It only makes things worse."

"Purse? Have you lost it?" said the Saucepan Man, anxiously.

"I said 'worse' not 'purse'," said Silky. "Come on! Let's go. Connie's dry now, but I can't get the ink-stains out of her dress."

They all began to climb the tree again, the Saucepan Man making a frightful noise. He began to sing his silly song.

27

"Two bangs for a pop-gun,
        Two . . ."

"Be quiet!" said Silky. "You'll wake Mister Watzisname. He's fast asleep. He went to bed very late last night, so he'll be tired. We won't wake him. We shall be a dreadful squash inside Moon-Face's house anyhow. Steal past his chair quietly. Saucepan, try not to make your kettles clang together."

"Yes, lovely weather," agreed Saucepan, mishearing again. They all stole past. Saucepan made a few clatters, but they didn't disturb Watzisname, who snored loudly and peacefully in his deck-chair on the broad bough of the tree outside his house. His mouth was wide open.

"I wonder people don't pop things in his mouth if he leaves it open like that," whispered Connie.

"People do," said Jo. "Moon-Face put some acorns in once. He was awfully angry. He really was. It's a wonder he doesn't get soaked with Dame Washalot's water, but he doesn't seem to. He always puts his chair well under that big branch."

They went on up the tree. In the distance they saw Dame Washalot, hanging out some clothes on boughs. "They blow away if she doesn't get someone to sit on them," said Silky to Connie. "So she pays the baby squirrels to sit patiently on each bit of washing she does till it's dry and she can take it in and iron it."

They saw the line of baby squirrels in the

distance. They looked sweet. Connie wanted to go nearer, but Jo said no, they really must go on; Moon-Face would be tired of waiting for them.

At last they came almost to the top of the tree. Connie was amazed when she looked down. The Faraway Tree rose higher than any other tree in the Enchanted Wood. Far below them waved the tops of other trees. Truly the Faraway Tree was amazing.

"Here we are, at Moon-Face's," said Jo, and he banged on the door. It flew open and Moon-Face looked out, his big round face one large smile.

"I thought you were never coming!" he said. "You *are* late!"

"We've brought this dirty little girl," said Saucepan, and he pushed Connie forward.

Moon-Face looked at her.

"She does look a bit dirty," he said, and smiled broadly. "I suppose she got into trouble with the Angry Pixie — and got some of Dame Washalot's water on her too! Never mind! Come along in and we'll have a good tea. I've got some Hot-Cold Goodies!"

"Whatever are they?" said Connie, and even the others hadn't heard of them.

They all went into Moon-Face's exciting house. It was really rather extraordinary. In the very middle was a large hole, with a pile of coloured cushions by it. Round the hole was Moon-Face's furniture, all curved to fit the roundness of the tree-trunk. There was a curious curved bed, a curved sofa, and a curved stove and chairs, all set

29

round the trunk inside the tree.

"It's very exciting," said Connie, looking round. "What's that hole in the middle?"

Nobody answered her. They were too busy looking at the lovely tea that Moon-Face had put ready on the curved table. They wanted to know what the Hot-Cold Goodies were like. They knew Pop Biscuits and Google Buns—but they didn't know Hot-Cold Goodies.

"What's this *hole*?" demanded Connie again, but no one bothered about her. She felt so curious that she went to the edge of the strange hole, and put her foot in it to see if there were steps down. She suddenly lost her balance, and stepped right into the hole! She sat down with a bump—and then, oh my goodness! she began to slide away at top speed down the hole that ran from the top of the tree to the bottom!

"Where's Connie?" said Jo, suddenly, looking round.

"Not here. That's good!" said Saucepan.

"She must have fallen down the Slippery-Slip!" said Silky. "Oh, poor Connie—she'll be at the bottom of the tree by now! We'll have to go down and fetch her!"

4.

Tea with Moon-Face

Connie was frightened when she found herself slipping down the hole in the tree. Usually people who used the Slippery-Slip had a cushion to sit on, but Connie hadn't. She slid down and down and round and round, faster and faster. She gasped, and her hair flew out behind her.

She came to the bottom of the tree, and her feet touched a little trapdoor set in the side there. It flew open and Connie shot out, landing on a soft tuft of moss, which the little folk grew there especially, so that anyone using the Tree-slide might land softly.

Connie landed on the moss and sat there, panting and frightened. She was at the bottom of the tree! The others were all at the top! They would be having tea together, laughing and joking. They wouldn't miss her. She would have to stay at the bottom of the tree till they came down again, and that might not be for ages.

"If I knew the way home I'd go," thought Connie. "But I don't. Oh — what's that?"

It was a red squirrel, dressed in an old jersey. He came out of a hole in the trunk, where he lived. He bounded over to Connie.

"Where's your cushion, please?" he said.

"What cushion?" said Connie.

"The one you slid down on," said the squirrel.

"I didn't slide down on one," said Connie.

"You must have," said the red squirrel, looking all round for a cushion. "People always do. Where have you put it? Don't be a naughty girl now. Let me have it. I always have to take them back to Moon-Face."

"I tell you I didn't have a cushion," said Connie, beginning to feel annoyed. "I just slid down on myself, and I got pretty warm."

She stood up. The squirrel looked at the back of her. "My! You've worn out the back of your frock, sliding down without a cushion," he said. "It's all in rags. Your petticoat is showing."

"Oh! This is a horrid afternoon!" said poor Connie. "I've been splashed with ink and soaked with soapy water, and now I've worn out the back of my frock."

The trap-door suddenly shot open again and out flew Moon-Face on one of his cushions. He shouted to Connie.

"I say! Didn't you like my party? Why did you rush off so quickly?"

"I fell down that silly hole," said Connie. "Look at the back of my frock."

"There's nothing to look at. You've worn it out, slipping down without a cushion," said Moon-Face. "Come on, I'll take you back. Look out—here comes a basket. It's one of Dame Washalot's biggest ones. I borrowed it from her to go back in. All right, red squirrel, don't take my cushion. I'll put it in the basket to sit on."

The red squirrel said good-bye and popped

back into his hole. Moon-Face caught the big
basket that came swinging down on a stout rope
and threw his yellow cushion into it. He helped
Connie in, tugged at the rope, and then up they
swung between the branches of the tree. Up and
up and up—past the Angry Pixie's, past the Owl's
home, past Mister Watzisname, still snoring, past
Dame Washalot, and right up to Moon-Face's
own house.

"Here we are!" he called to Jo and the Saucepan
Man, who were busy tugging at the rope, to
bring up the basket. "Thanks so much."

Everyone was amused to see that the bottom
part of poor Connie's dress was gone. "She's

ragged now as well as dirty," said Saucepan, sounding quite pleased. He didn't like Connie. "I wonder what will happen to her next."

"Nothing, I hope," said Connie, scowling at him.

"Soap? Yes, you do look as if you want a bit of soap," said Saucepan, mis-hearing as usual. "And a needle and cotton too."

"Now, stop it, Saucepan!" said Silky. "I've never known you so quarrelsome. Come and eat the Hot-Cold Goodies. Nobody's had any yet."

They went into Moon-Face's curved home, and sat down again. Connie tried not to go near the hole. She was very much afraid of falling down it again. She took a Hot-Cold Goodie. It was like a very, very big chocolate.

Hot-Cold Goodies were peculiar. You put them into your mouth and sucked. As soon as you had sucked the chocolate part off, you came to what seemed like a layer of ice-cream."

"Oooh! Ice-cream!" said Jo, sucking hard. "Cold as can be. Golly, it's too cold to bear! It's getting colder and colder. Moon-Face, I'll have to spit out my goodie, it's too cold for me."

But just as he said that the Hot-Cold Goodie stopped being cold and got hot. At first it was pleasantly warm, and then it got very hot.

"It's almost burning me!" said Bessie. "Oh— now it's gone ice-cold again. Moon-Face, what extraordinary things. Wherever did you get them?"

"I bought them from a witch who popped down from the Land of Marvels to-day," said Moon-

Face, grinning. "Funny, aren't they?"

"Yes—awfully exciting, and delicious to taste, once you get used to them changing from cold to hot and hot to cold," said Bessie. "I'll have another."

"What land did you say was at the top of the Tree to-day?" asked Silky. "The Land of Marvels? Oh yes—I went there last year, I remember."

"What was it like?" asked Fanny.

"Marvellous," said Silky. "All wonders and marvels. There's a ladder that hasn't any top—you go on and on climbing up it, and you never reach the top—and a tree that sings whenever the wind blows—a cat that tells your fortune—and a silver ball that takes you all round the world and back in the wink of an eye—well, I can't tell you all the marvels there are."

"I'd like to go and see them," said Jo.

"You can't," said Silky. "The Land moves on to-day. It would be dangerous to go there now because it might move on at any moment. Then you'd be stuck in the Land of Marvels."

"I don't believe a word of it," said Connie.

"She doesn't believe in anything magic," explained Jo, seeing that Silky looked rather surprised. "Don't take any notice of her, Silky. She'll believe all right soon."

"I shall *not*," said Connie. "I'm beginning to think this is all a horrid dream."

"Well, go home and go to bed and dream your dream there," said Jo, getting tired of Connie.

"I will," said Connie, getting up, offended. "I'll

climb down the tree myself, and ask that kind red squirrel to see me home. This is a horrid party."

The silly girl went to the door, opened it, went out and banged it shut. The others stared at one another.

"Is she always like that?" asked Moon-Face.

"Yes," said Jo. "She's an only child, and very spoilt, you know. Wants her own way always, and turns up her nose at everything. I'd better fetch her back."

"No, don't," said Moon-Face. "She can't come to any harm. Let her climb down the tree if she wants to. I only hope she peeps in at the Angry Pixie's again. When I went past in the basket he was writing a letter again, but with red ink this time."

"Then Connie will probably get *red* spots on her dress now!" said Fanny.

But Connie hadn't gone down the Tree. She stood outside on a branch, sulking. She looked down the tree and saw Dame Washalot busy washing again. Silly old woman! Connie didn't feel as if she wanted to go near her, in case she got water all over her again. She looked upwards.

She was nearly at the top of the tree. She thought it would be fun to climb right up to the top, and look down on the forest. What a long way she would see!

She climbed upwards. She came to the top of the tree — and to her great astonishment the last branch of all touched the clouds! Yes — it went straight up into a vast white cloud that hung, floating, over the top of the Tree.

"Queer," said Connie, looking up into the purple hole made by the tree-branch in the cloud. "Shall I go up there—into the cloud? Yes—I will."

She went up the last branch—and to her still greater amazement there was a little ladder leading through the thickness of the cloud from the branch. A ladder!

Connie was full of great curiosity. She could hardly bear to wait to see what was at the top of the ladder. She climbed it—and suddenly her head poked right through the cloud, and into a new and different Land altogether!

"Well!" said Connie, in surprise. "So the children told the truth. There *is* a Land at the top of the Faraway Tree—and can I really be dreaming?"

She climbed up into the Land. It was queer. There was a curious humming noise in the air. Strange people walked quickly past, some looking like witches, and some like goblins. They took no notice of Connie.

"The Land is moving on!" cried one goblin to another. "It's on the move again. Where shall we go to next?"

And then the Land of Marvels moved away from the top of the Tree—and took poor Connie with it!

5.

Off to Jack-and-the-Bean-Stalk

Jo, Bessie, Fanny and the others went on with their tea. They finished the Hot-Cold Goodies, then they started on some pink jelly that Moon-Face had made in the shape of animals. They were so nicely made that it seemed quite a pity to eat them.

"We'd better save some for Connie, hadn't we?" said Bessie. "Let's see if she's outside the door. I expect she's standing there, sulking."

Moon-Face opened the door. There was no one there. He called loudly, "Connie! Connie!"

There was no answer. "She's gone down the Tree, I should think," he said. "I'll just yell down to Dame Washalot and see if she saw her."

So he shouted down to the old dame. But Dame Washalot shook her head. "No," she shouted back, "no one has passed by here since you came up in the basket, Moon-Face. No one at all."

"Funny!" said Moon-Face, going to tell the others. "Where's she gone, then?"

"Up through the cloud?" said Silky.

"No—surely she wouldn't have done that by herself," said Jo, in alarm. "Look, Moon-Face! There's the red squirrel who wants to speak to you."

The red squirrel came in, trying to hide a hole in his old jersey. "I heard you calling Connie,

Mister Moon-Face," he said. "Well, she's gone up the ladder through the cloud. I expect she's in the Land of Marvels. I saw her go."

"Good gracious!" cried Jo, jumping up in alarm. "Why, the Land is ready to leave here at any minute, didn't you say, Silky? What a silly she is! We'd better go and get her back at once."

"I thought I heard the humming noise that means any Land is moving on," said Moon-Face, looking troubled. "I don't believe we can save her. I'll pop up the ladder and see."

He climbed up the highest branch and went up the ladder. But there was nothing to be seen at all except swirling, misty cloud. He came down again.

"The Land of Marvels is gone," he said. "And the next Land hasn't even come yet. I don't know what it will be, either. Well—Connie's gone with the Land of Marvels. She *would* do a silly thing like that!"

Bessie went pale. "But what can we do about it?" she said. "Whatever can we do? We're in charge of her, you know. We simply can't let her go like this. We must find her somehow."

"How *can* we?" said Silky. "You know that once a Land has moved on, it doesn't come back for ages. Connie will have to stay there. I don't see that it matters, anyway. She's not a very nice person."

"Oh Silky, you don't understand!" said Jo. He looked very worried. "She's our friend. And though she's silly and annoying at times, we have to look after her and help her. How can we get to her?"

"You can't," said Moon-Face.

Saucepan had been trying to follow what had been said, his face looking very earnest. He didn't like Connie, and he thought it was a very good thing she had gone off in the Land of Marvels. But he did know a way of getting there, and he badly wanted to tell the others.

But they all talked at once, and he couldn't get a word in! So, in despair he clashed his saucepans and kettles together so violently that everyone jumped and stared round at him.

"He wants to say something," said Jo. "Go on, out with it, Saucepan."

Saucepan came out with it in a rush. "*I* know how to get to the Land of Marvels without waiting for it to arrive here again," he said. "You can get to it from the Land of Giants, which joins on to it."

"Well, I don't see how that helps us," said Moon-Face. "We don't know how to get to the Land of Giants either, silly!"

"No, it's not hilly," said Saucepan, going all deaf again. "It's quite flat. The giants have made it flat by walking about on it with their enormous feet."

"What *is* he talking about?" said Bessie. "Saucepan, stop talking about the geography of Giantland and tell us how to get there."

"How to get there, did you say?" asked Saucepan, putting his hand behind his left ear.

"YES!" yelled everyone.

"Well, that's easy," said Saucepan, beaming round. 'Same way as Jack-and-the-Bean-Stalk did, of course. Up the Bean-Stalk!"

Everyone stared at Saucepan in silence. They all had heard of Jack-and-the-Bean-Stalk, of course, and how he climbed up the Bean-Stalk into Giantland.

"But where's the Bean-Stalk?" asked Jo at last.

"Where Jack lives," said Saucepan, suddenly hearing well again. "I know him quite well. Married a princess and lives in a castle."

"I never knew that he was an old friend of yours," said Moon-Face. "How did you come to know him?"

"I sold him a lot of saucepans and kettles," said the Saucepan Man. "He was giving an enormous dinner-party, and they hadn't enough things to cook everything in. So I came along just at the right moment and sold him everything I'd got. Very lucky for him."

"And for you too," grinned Moon-Face. "Well, you'd better take us to your Jack, Saucepan. We'll go up the Bean-Stalk, and try and rescue that silly little Connie."

"We'd better not *all* go," said Jo, looking round at the little company.

"I must go to show you the way," said Saucepan, who loved making a journey.

"And I must go, of course," said Moon-Face.

"And I shall come with you to look after you," said Silky, firmly. "You always get into such

41

silly scrapes if I'm not there to see to you."

"And I shall certainly come, because I was really in charge of Connie," said Jo.

"And *we're* not going to be left out of an adventure like this!" said Bessie at once. "Are we, Fanny?"

"Well—it looks as if we're all going then," said Moon-Face. "All right, let's go. But don't let's get caught by any giants, for goodness' sake. *Must* we go through Giantland to get to the Land of Marvels, Saucepan?"

"Bound to," said Saucepan, cheerfully. "The giants won't hurt you. They're quite harmless nowadays. Well, come on! Down the tree we go, and then to the other end of the Wood."

So down the Tree they went, and the red squirrel bounded with them to the bottom. They wished they could skip down as he did—it didn't take him more than half a minute to get up or down!

They reached the bottom, and then thought how silly they were not to have gone down the Slippery-Slip!

"It shows how worried we are, not to have thought of that!" said Bessie. "Which way now, Saucepan?"

Saucepan set off down a narrow, winding path. "This way, look—under this hedge, and across this field. We've got to get to the station," he said.

"Station? What station?" said Jo, in astonishment.

"To get the train for Jack-and-the-Bean-Stalk's

castle," said Saucepan. "How stupid you are, all of a sudden, Jo!"

They came suddenly to a small station set under a row of poplar trees. A train came puffing in, looking very like an old wooden one with carriages that the children had at home. They got in, and it went off, puffing hard as if it was out of breath.

They passed through many queer little stations, but didn't stop. "I said 'Bean-Stalk Castle' to the engine, so it will go straight there," said Saucepan.

The other passengers didn't seem to mind going to Bean-Stalk Castle at all. They sat and talked or read, and took no notice of the others.

The train suddenly stopped and hooted. "Here we are," said Saucepan. "Come on, everyone."

They got out on to a tiny platform. The engine gave another hoot and went rattling off.

"There's Jack! Hi there, Jack!" suddenly yelled Saucepan, and rushed towards a sturdy young man in the distance. They shook hands, all Saucepan's kettles and pans rattling excitedly.

"What a pleasure, what a pleasure!" cried Jack. "Who are all these people? Have they come to stay with me? I'll go and tell the Princess to make up extra beds at once."

"No, don't do that," said Moon-Face. "We haven't come to stay. We just want to know—may we please use your Bean-Stalk, Jack?"

"It hasn't grown this year yet," said Jack. "I forgot to plant any beans, you see. Also, the giants were a bit of a nuisance last year, always shouting rude things down the Bean-Stalk to me."

"Oh!" said Jo, staring at Jack in dismay. "What a pity! We particularly wanted to go up your Bean-Stalk."

"Well—I can plant the beans now, and they'll grow," said Jack. "They're magic ones, you know. They grow as you watch them."

"Oh, good!" said Moon-Face. "Could you plant some, do you think? We'd be most awfully obliged."

"Certainly," said Jack, and he felt about in his pocket. "I'd do anything to help old Saucepan. His kettles and saucepans are still going strong in my kitchen—never wear out at all. Now—wherever did I put those beans?"

The others watched anxiously as he turned a queer collection of things out of his pockets. At last came three or four mouldy-looking beans.

"Here we are," said Jack. "I'll just press them into the earth—so—and now we'll watch them grow. Stand back, please, because they sometimes shoot up at a great pace!"

6.

To the Land of Giants

Everyone watched the ground in which Jack had buried the beans. At first nothing happened. Then a sort of hillock came, as if a mole was working there. The hillock split and up came some Bean-Stalks, putting out two bean-leaves. Then other leaves sprang from the centre of the stalk, and pointed upwards. Then yet others came, and the Bean-Stalks grew higher and higher.

"Queer!" said Bessie, watching them grow up and up. "They don't even need a pole to climb up, Jack. Is that how they grew when you first planted them, years ago, to climb up to Giantland?"

"Just the same," said Jack. "Look—you can't even see the tops of them now! It's amazing how they spring up, isn't it? Look how thick and strong the stems have grown, too!"

So they had. They were like the trunks of young trees.

"Have they reached Giantland yet?" asked Moon-Face, squinting up.

"Can't tell till you climb up," said Jack. "I'd come with you, but I've got visitors coming—and the Princess isn't at all pleased if I'm not there to greet them. So I'd better go now."

He shook hands politely all round, and was very pleased when the Saucepan Man presented him with an extra large kettle in return for his kindness. Bessie was glad to see him taking the kettle.

Up the Bean-Stalk they all went. It was not at all difficult, for there were plenty of strong leaf-stalks to tread on and to haul themselves up by. But it did seem a very, very long way to the top!

"I believe we're going to the Moon!" said Jo, panting. "We shall see the Man in the Moon peeping at us over the top!"

But they didn't go to the Moon. They went to

Giantland, of course, because the beans never grew up to anywhere else. The topmost shoots waved over Giantland, and the children and the others rolled off them and lay panting on the ground to rest.

"Gracious! I couldn't have climbed any further!" said Bessie, trying to get her breath. "Oh my, what in the world is that, Jo?"

"It's an earthquake!" cried Fanny. "Can't you feel the earth trembling and quaking?"

"Here's a mountain coming on top of us!" shouted Jo, and pulled the girls down a nearby hole.

Saucepan peered down, laughing. "No earthquake and no mountain!" he said. "Just an ordinary giant coming along, whose foot-steps shake the ground."

The noise and the earthquake grew worse and then passed. The giant had gone by. Everyone breathed again and crept out of the hole.

"I suppose that's a rabbit-hole we were in, where giant rabbits live," said Bessie.

"No—a worm-hole, where giant worms live," said Moon-Face. "I saw one down at the bottom, like an enormous snake."

"Oh dear—I shan't go down a hole like that again!" said Fanny. But she did, when another earthquake and walking mountain appeared! It was another giant, tall as the sky, his great feet shaking the earth below.

"Come on!" said Moon-Face, when the second giant had gone safely by. "We must hurry. And for goodness' sake pop out of the way if another giant comes by, because we don't want to be squashed like currants under his feet."

The third giant stopped when he came near them. He bent down, and the children saw that he wore glasses on his enormous nose. They looked as large as shop-window panes!

"Ha! What are these little creatures?" said the giant, in a voice that boomed like a thunderstorm. "Beetles, I should think — or ants! Most extraordinary, I have never seen any like them before!"

There was no hole to slip down. The children saw that the giant was trying to pick one of them up! An enormous hand, with fingers as thick as young tree-trunks came down near them.

Everyone was too scared to move, and there was nowhere to hide, except for a large dandelion growing as tall as a tree, nearby. But Saucepan had a bright idea. He undid his biggest saucepan, and clapped it on the top of the giant's thumb; it fitted it exactly, and stuck there.

The giant gave a loud cry of surprise, and lifted up his hand. He stood up to see this funny thing that had suddenly appeared on his thumb, and Saucepan yelled to everyone.

"To the dandelion, quick! Hurry!"

They rushed to the tall dandelion plant. One of the heads floated high above them, a beautiful ripe, dandelion "clock," full of seeds ready to fly off in the wind.

Saucepan shook the stalk violently, and some of

the seeds flew off, floating in the air on their parachute of hairs.

"Catch the stalks of the seeds, catch them, and let the wind float you away!" yelled Saucepan. "The giant won't guess we're off with the dandelion seeds."

So each of them caught hold of a dandelion seed. Fanny got two, and held on tightly! Then the wind blew, and the plumy seeds floated high in the air, taking everyone with them. They saw the giant kneel down on the ground to look for the funny creatures that had put the saucepan on his thumb—but then they were off and away, floating high in the breeze.

"Keep together, keep together!" called Moon-Face, grabbing Silky's hand. "We don't want to be blown apart, all over Giantland. We'll never meet again! Take hands when you get near."

Fanny was nearly lost, because she had hold of two seeds instead of one, and was blown higher than the others. But Jo managed to grab her feet and pulled her down beside him. He made her leave go one of her dandelion seeds, and took her hand firmly.

They were now all linking hands in pairs, and kept together well. They floated high over Giantland, marvelling at the enormous castles there, the great gardens and tall trees.

"Even the Faraway Tree would look small here!" said Bessie.

"Look—there's the boundary between the Land of Marvels, and Giantland!" suddenly cried

Saucepan, almost letting go his dandelion seed in his excitement. "I'd no idea we would get there so soon. What a wall!"

It was indeed a marvellous wall. It rose steadily up, so high that it seemed there was no end to it, and it shimmered and shook as if it were made of water.

"It's a magic wall," said Saucepan. "I remember seeing it before. No giant can get in or out, over or under it, because it's painted with Giant-Proof paint."

"What's that?" asked Jo, shouting.

"Giant-Proof paint can only be bought in the Land of Marvels," explained Saucepan. "Anything painted with it keeps giants away, just like the smell of camphor keeps moths away. It's marvellous. No giant can come within yards of anything painted with that silvery magic paint. I only wish I had some!"

"Well—how are *we* to get over or under this wall?" said Moon-Face, as they floated near. "It may be Giant-Proof, but it looks as if it would be Us-Proof too!"

"Oh no—we can go right through it," said Silky. "You'll see that as soon as we get right up to it, it won't be there! It's only Giant-Proof."

This sounded extraordinary, but Silky's words were quite true. When they reached the wall, it gave one last shimmer—and was gone! The children floated right down into the Land of Marvels, where everything was the right size. It was a great relief to see things properly again, and not to have to crane your neck to see if a flower was a daisy or a pimpernel!

They floated to the ground, let go their dandelion seeds, which gradually became the right size, once they were away from Giantland, and looked round them.

"There's the ladder-without-a-top," said Silky, pointing. "No one has ever climbed beyond the three thousandth rung, because they get so tired. And there's the Tree-That-Sings. It's singing now."

So it was — a whispery, beautiful song, all about the sun and the wind and rain. The children could understand it perfectly, though the tree did not use any words they knew. It just stood there and poured out its song in tree-language.

"I could listen to that for ages," said Jo. "But we really must get on. Now — we must all hunt for Connie. Let's shout for her, shall we? Now — altogether — shout!"

They shouted. "CON-NEE! CON-NEE! CON-NEE!"

An old woman nearby looked crossly at them. "Be quiet!" she said. "Making such a noise! I've a good mind to change you all into a thunderstorm. Then you can make as much noise as you like! It's bad enough to have *one* child here, making a fuss and yelling and screaming, without having a whole crowd!"

"Oh — have you seen a child here?" said Jo, at once, in his politest voice. "Where is she, please? We are trying to look for her."

"She went up the Ladder-That-Has-No-Top," said the old woman. "And she hasn't come down. I hope she stays up there for good!"

"Oh—bother Connie!" groaned Jo. "Now we shall have to do a bit more climbing, and see how far up the ladder she's gone! Come on!"

So off they all went to the shining ladder, that stretched from the ground up and up and up. No top could be seen. It was an extraordinary thing.

"I'll go," said Moon-Face. "I'm not tired, and all you others are. I'll bring Connie down. I don't expect she's gone farther than the hundredth rung!"

He went up the ladder, and the others sat down at the bottom waiting. They waited and they waited. Why ever didn't Moon-Face come?

7.

Up the Ladder-That-Has-No-Top

Jo and the others waited and waited, looking up the ladder every now and again. Bessie got impatient and wandered off to look at some of the marvels. Jo called her back.

"Bessie! Don't go wandering off by yourself, for goodness' sake! We don't want to lose *you*, as soon as we find Connie. We'll have a look at the Marvels when Moon-Face brings Connie back."

"Well, he's such ages up the ladder," complained

Bessie. "I did want to go and see the Cat that Tells Fortunes. He might tell me how we are to get back home!"

"Back through Giantland, I suppose," said Silky.

"I *wish* Moon-Face would come!" sighed Fanny, looking up the ladder for the twentieth time. "What *is* he doing up there? Surely Connie can't have climbed very far!"

Moon-Face had gone up a good way. He climbed steadily, looking up every now and again, hoping to see Connie. At last he saw a pair of feet, and he gave a yell.

"Connie! I've come to rescue you! It's Moon-Face coming up the ladder!"

The feet didn't move. They were big feet, and it suddenly struck Moon-Face that they were too big for Connie. He looked above the feet, and saw a goblin looking down at him.

"Oh!" said Moon-Face. "I thought you were Connie. Let me pass, please."

"Can't think why there's so much traffic on this ladder to-day," said the goblin, grumbling as he sat to one side. He had big feet, big hands, a big head, and a very small body, so he looked rather queer. On his knees he balanced a big tin of paint, out of which stuck a paint-brush.

"What are *you* doing up here?" asked Moon-Face. "Painting or something?"

"I'm the goblin painter who made that wall Giant-Proof," said the goblin. He pointed to where the wall between Giantland and the Land of

Marvels shimmered and quivered like a heat-haze. "But I got into trouble with Witch Wily, who used to go and shop in Giantland. I splashed some of my paint over her, and that meant she was Giant-Proof too. No giant in Giantland could go near her, so she couldn't do any more shopping!"

"So she chased you, I suppose, to put a spell on you, and you rushed up the Ladder-That-Has-No-Top!" said Moon-Face, sitting down beside him to peer at his paint. "Bad luck! Why doesn't she chase you up here?"

"She doesn't like climbing," said the goblin. "But she's waiting down there at the bottom, I'm sure of it."

"She isn't," said Moon-Face. "I've just come up, and there was no witch down there. You go on down now, and see. I'm sure you can slip off and escape."

"She said she'd empty my Giant-Proof paint all over me if she caught me," said the goblin, dolefully.

"Well, leave it here with me," said Moon-Face. "I'll bring it down for you. Then, if the witch *is* at the bottom it won't matter, because you won't have your paint with you."

"Right!" said the goblin, cheering up. He tied the handle of his paint-tin to a rung of the ladder, and began to go down. Moon-Face suddenly remembered Connie, and he called down to the goblin.

"Hi! Just a minute! Have you seen a little girl go up the ladder?"

53

"Oh yes," said the goblin, stopping. "A dirty little girl, very frightened. She was crying. She pushed past me very rudely indeed. I didn't like her."

"Oh, that's Connie all right," said Moon-Face, and he began to climb up again. "I hope she's not gone too far up. She really is a nuisance."

He lost sight of the goblin. He went on climbing up and up, and at last he heard a miserable voice above him. It was Connie's.

"I can't climb any farther! This ladder doesn't lead anywhere. I can't climb down because that imp will smack me. I shall have to stay here for the rest of my life. Hoo-hoo-hoo!"

Connie sobbed, and two or three tears splashed down on Moon-Face's head. He rubbed them off. Then he saw Connie's feet above him.

"Hi, Connie!" he called.

Connie gave a shriek and almost fell off the ladder. Moon-Face felt it wobbling. "Oh! Oh! Who is it?" cried Connie, and began to climb hurriedly up the ladder again, afraid that the imp was after her.

This was too much for Moon-Face. Here he had gone all the way to the Land of Marvels, through Giantland, and up goodness knows how many rungs of the ladder — and just as he had found Connie she began climbing up and up again. He caught firmly hold of one of her ankles. She screamed.

"Let go! I shall bite you! Let go!"

"You come down," commanded Moon-Face.

"I've come to take you back home, you silly girl. You've caused us all a lot of trouble. Come on down! I'm Moon-Face."

Connie sat down on the ladder in the greatest relief. She put her arms round Moon-Face as he came up beside her, and hugged him.

"Moon-Face! I was never in my life so pleased to see anyone. Tell me how you got here."

"No," said Moon-Face, wriggling away. "There's no time. The others are waiting and waiting at the foot of the ladder. Come on down, you silly girl!"

"But there's an imp . . ." began Connie.

"No, there isn't," said Moon-Face, beginning to wonder how many other people there were sitting on the ladder, afraid to go down because they thought someone was watching for them at the bottom. "There's no imp and no witch and no nothing. Only Jo, Bessie, Fanny, Silky and Saucepan. Come on, do!"

He made Connie climb down below him. "Now, if you don't climb down pretty fast, I shall be treading on your fingers!" he said, and that made Connie squeal and climb down much more quickly than she had meant to. Down and down they went, down and down. And, at last, there they were on the ground!

The others crowded round them. "Moon-Face! We thought you were never coming!"

"Connie! Are you all right?"

"An imp came hurrying down, but he wouldn't stop to tell us anything!"

"Moon-Face, what have you got in that tin?"

Moon-Face showed them the tin of Giant-Proof paint he had brought down with him. He had untied it from the ladder when he came to it. He told them about the imp.

Connie was longing to tell her adventures, too. She told them at last.

"When I got here, into this land, I wandered about a bit," she said. "And I came to the cat that could tell fortunes, so I asked him to tell me mine. And he told me all kinds of nasty things he said would happen to me, so I smacked him hard, and he hissed at me and ran away."

"You naughty girl!" said Silky.

"Well, he shouldn't have said nasty things to me," said Connie. "Then an imp, whose cat it was, came after me with a broom, and said he would sweep me up and put me into a dust-bin. Horrid creature!"

The others laughed. They thought Connie deserved all she got. "So I suppose you shot up the ladder to escape and didn't dare to come down?" said Jo.

"Yes," said Connie. "And I was so pleased to see Moon-Face. I don't like this land. And I don't like the Faraway Tree either, or the Enchanted Wood."

"Or me, or Bessie, or Fanny, or Silky, or Moon-Face, or Saucepan, I suppose?" said Jo. "Pleasant child, aren't you? I feel that if I were an imp I would certainly take a broom to you. Well, what about going home? It's getting late."

"Oh dear — have we got to go through Giant-land again?" said Silky. "I didn't much like those enormous giants. I'm afraid of their great big feet."

"Yes, we've got to go through Giantland," said Moon-Face. "But I've got an idea. I'll splash you all with a few drops of Giant-Proof paint! Then no giant can come near us. We'll be like that wall — giant-proof!"

"Oh, what a good idea!" said Bessie. So Moon-Face quickly dabbed a few drops of paint on each of them. The places he dabbed shone and shimmered queerly, like the wall. The children laughed.

"We look queer. Never mind — if it keeps the giants away from us, it will be fine."

They made their way to the shining wall, which disappeared as they walked through it, and re-appeared again as soon as they were on the other side. Then they began to walk cautiously through Giantland, to find the top of the Bean-Stalk.

Many giants were out, taking an evening walk. Some of them saw the children and exclaimed in surprise. They knelt down to pick them up.

But they couldn't touch them! The Giant-Proof paint prevented any giant from getting too near, and no matter how they tried they couldn't get hold of any of the little company.

"This is jolly good stuff, this paint," said Jo, pleased. "It was a good idea of yours, Moon-Face."

"Look—there's the top of the Bean-Stalk," said Silky, joyfully. "Now we shan't be long!"

The giants followed them to the Bean-Stalk. The children and the others climbed down as quickly as they could, half afraid that the giants might shake the Bean-Stalk so that they would fall off. But they didn't. They just called rudely down after them.

They got to the ground and sighed for joy. "My goodness, we're late!" said Jo, looking at his watch. "We must make for home at once. Where's that train?"

Soon they were in the queer little train. They got out at the Enchanted Wood, said good-bye to Moon-Face, Silky and Saucepan, and made their way home. Connie was very tired.

"Well—I suppose you didn't enjoy the party very much?" said Jo to Connie. "And what about the Faraway Tree and the people there? Do you believe in them now?"

"I suppose I shall have to," said Connie. "But I didn't like any of them much, except Moon-Face. I can't bear Saucepan."

"He doesn't seem to like you, either," said Bessie. "Well, Connie—you don't need to come with us again if you don't want to. We can leave you behind!"

But that didn't please Connie! No—she meant to go where the others went. *She* wasn't going to be left out!

8.

The Faraway Tree Again

Mother wasn't very pleased to see how dirty, ink-spotted and ragged Connie's clothes were when she came back with the others.

"I shan't let you go with the others to the Faraway Tree again if you can't keep yourself cleaner than this," she said, crossly. Connie was not used to being talked to like this, and she burst into tears.

The children's mother popped Connie's clothes into the wash-tub and said, "To-morrow you will iron and mend these clothes, Connie. Stop that noise, or I shall send you to bed without any supper."

All the children were tired, and fell asleep as soon as their heads touched the pillow. When Connie woke up, she remembered all that had happened the day before, and wondered if she could possibly have dreamt it. It seemed so queer when she thought about it.

"Are we going to the Faraway Tree to-day again?" she asked Jo, when they were all at breakfast.

Jo shook his head.

"No. We've got lots of work to do. And anyway you didn't like it, or the people there, so we shall go alone."

Connie looked as if she was going to burst into tears. Then she remembered that tears didn't seem to bother anyone here, and she blinked them away. "What Land will be at the top of the Tree this week?" she asked.

"Don't know," said Jo. "Anyway, we're not going, Connie. We've had enough travelling this week!"

The next two days it rained so hard that Mother wouldn't let the children go out. They heard nothing from their friends in the Faraway Tree.

The next day shone sunny and the sky was a lovely blue. "As if it had been washed clean by all the rain," said Fanny. "Let's go to the Enchanted Wood. May we, Mother?"

"Well, yes, I should think so," said Mother. "I badly want a new saucepan, a nice little one, for boiling milk. You might go and ask the Saucepan Man to sell me one. Here is the money."

"Oh, lovely!" said Bessie, overjoyed at the thought of visiting the Faraway Tree-Folk again. "We'll go this morning."

"I'm going too," said Connie.

"You're not," said Jo. "You're going to stay at home like a good girl, and help Mother. You'll like that."

"Indeed I shan't!" said Connie. "Don't be mean. Take me with you."

"Well, it's no fun to take you," said Jo. "You haven't any manners, and you don't do what you're told, and people don't like you. You're far better at home. Anyway, you don't believe in anything in the Enchanted Wood, so why do you want to come?"

"Because I don't want to be left out," wailed Connie. "Let me come. I'll be good. I'll have nice manners. I'll like everyone."

"Well, you won't go in that nice little frock," said Jo's mother, firmly. "I'm not going to have you spoil another. If you go, you must borrow an old cotton frock of Fanny's. They're rather patched, but that won't matter."

Connie didn't want to wear Fanny's old frock, but she went to put it on. She couldn't bear being left out, and if the others were going off to the Wood she felt she really must go too. Soon she came back again in Fanny's old washed-out frock.

"You look sensible now," said Jo. "Very sensible. It won't even matter if you go down the Slippery-Slip without a cushion again. That material won't wear out in a hurry. Come on, everybody!"

They set off, Jo jingling the money for the saucepan in his shorts' pocket. They jumped over the ditch and landed in the Enchanted Wood. At once everything seemed magic and different. Connie felt excited again. She was longing to see Moon-Face, who, since he had rescued her from the Land of Marvels seemed to her to be a real hero.

They came to the Faraway Tree. It was so hot that the children didn't feel like climbing up. "We'll go up on cushions," said Jo. "We'll send the red squirrel up to tell Moon-Face to send some down on ropes."

He whistled a little tune and the red squirrel popped out of his hole. "Your jersey is getting so holey you won't be able to keep it on soon!" said Bessie.

"I know," said the squirrel. "But I don't know how to darn."

"I'll darn it for you one day," said Bessie. "I'm a good darner. Now, squirrel, go on up to Moon-Face, there's a dear, and ask him to send down four cushions on ropes. It's really too hot to climb up to-day."

The red squirrel bounded up the tree as light as a feather, his plumy tail waving behind him. The children sat down and waited, watching the queer little folk that trotted up and down the big tree, going about their business.

Soon there came a rustling of leaves, and down through the branches came four fat cushions, tied firmly to ropes. "Here we are," said Jo, jumping up. "Moon-Face has been jolly quick. Choose a cushion, Connie, and sit on it. Hold the rope tightly, give it three jerks, and up you'll go!"

It was exciting. Connie sat on the big, soft cushion, held on to the rope, and gave it three tugs. The rope was hauled up from above, and Connie went swinging upwards between the branches. She saw the Tree was growing apricots that day. She wondered if they were ripe.

She picked one and it was most deliciously sweet and juicy. She thought she would pick another, but by that time the Tree was growing acorns, which was most disappointing.

Soon everyone was on the broad branch outside Moon-Face's house. He was there with Mister Watzisname, pulling hard at the ropes.

"Hallo!" said Mister Watzisname, beaming at the children. "Haven't seen you for a long time."

"You've always been asleep when we've come here," said Jo. "Watzisname, this is Connie."

"Ah—how do you do?" said Watzisname. "Is this the little girl Saucepan was telling me about? She doesn't look so dirty and ragged as he said."

"*Well!*" began Connie, indignantly. "Fancy Saucepan saying . . ."

"Now, don't lose your temper," said Jo. "After all, you *did* look dirty and ragged the other day. Where *is* Saucepan, Moon-Face? I want to buy something from him."

"He's gone up into the Land at the top of the Tree," said Moon-Face. "He heard that there was an old friend of his there, Little Miss Muffet, and he wanted to go and see her. She once gave him some curds and whey when he was very hungry, and he has never forgotten it. It was the only time in his life he ever tasted curds and whey."

"Oh!" said Jo. "Well, what Land is up there this week, then?"

"The Land of Nursery Rhyme," said Moon-Face. "So Watzisname says, anyway. You went up, didn't you, Watzisname, and saw Little Tommy Tucker, and Little Jack Horner?"

"Yes," said Watzisname. "Quite an interesting

Land. All sorts of friendly people there."

"Let's go up and find Saucepan!" said Bessie. "It would be fun. It's quite a harmless Land, that's plain. Goodness knows how long Saucepan will be up there with Little Miss Muffet. Maybe he's feasting on curds and whey again, and won't be back for days!"

"Oh—do let's go!" said Connie. "And Moon-Face, dear Moon-Face, you come too."

"Don't call me 'Dear Moon-Face'," said Moon-Face. "You're not a friend of mine yet."

"Oh!" said Connie, who was so used to being fussed and spoilt by everyone that she couldn't understand anybody not liking her.

"I think it would be rather fun to go up and see the Nursery Rhyme people," said Jo. "Come on —let's go now. We could get a saucepan from the old Saucepan Man whilst we are there, and take it back with us."

"Well, come along, then," said Moon-Face, and led the way up the topmost branch of the tree. One by one they climbed it, came to the little ladder that led through the cloud, and found themselves in yet another land.

"The Land of the Nursery Rhyme Folk," said Bessie, looking round. "Well—we ought to know most of the people here, though they won't know us! I wonder where Saucepan is. He could introduce us to everyone."

"We'll ask where Little Miss Muffet lives," said Moon-Face. "Look—that must be Jack Horner over there, carrying a pie!"

"Ask him where Miss Muffet is," said Fanny. So they went over to where a fat little boy was just about to make a hole in his pie with his thumb.

"Please, where is Miss Muffet?" asked Jo.

"Over the other side of the hill," said Jack Horner, pointing with a juicy thumb. "Look out for her spider — he's pretty fierce to-day!"

9.

Nursery Rhyme Land

"What did he mean — look out for the spider?" asked Connie, looking round rather fearfully.

"Well, you know that a spider keeps coming and sitting down beside Miss Muffet whenever she eats her curds and whey, don't you?" said Jo. "We've just got to look out for it."

"I'm afraid of spiders," said Connie, looking ready to cry.

"You would be!" said Jo. "You're just the kind of person who's afraid of bats and moths and spiders and everything. Don't be silly. Go back if you'd rather not come with us."

"All the same — it may be rather a *big* spider," said Fanny.

Connie looked even more alarmed.

The children, Moon-Face and Watzisname walked to the hill, went up it, and stood at the top. Nursery Rhyme Land was nice. Its houses and cottages were thatched, and the little gardens were gay and flowery. The children felt that they knew everyone they met.

"Here's Tommy Tucker!" whispered Fanny, as a little boy hurried by, singing loudly in a clear, sweet voice. He heard her whisper and turned.

"Do you know me?" he asked in surprise. "I don't know you."

"*Are* you Tommy Tucker?" asked Bessie. "Were you going to sing for your supper?"

"Of course not. It's morning," said Tommy. "I sing for my supper at night. I was just practising a bit then. Do you sing for *your* supper?"

"No. We just have it anyhow, without singing," said Jo.

"You're lucky," said Tommy. "Nobody will give me any if I don't sing. It's a good thing I've got a nice voice!"

He went off singing like a blackbird again. The others watched him, and then saw someone else coming along crying bitterly. A bigger boy was slapping him hard. Behind the two came a thin cat, its fur wet and draggled.

"Hi! Stop hitting that boy!" cried Jo, who didn't like to see a smaller boy being hit by a bigger one. "Hit someone your own size!"

"Mind your own business," said the big boy. "Johnny Thin deserves all he gets. You don't know what a bad boy he is!"

"Johnny Thin! Oh, isn't he the boy who put the cat down the well?" cried Fanny. "Then you must be Johnny Stout, who pulled her out!"

"Yes—and there's the cat, poor thing," said Johnny Stout. "*Now* don't you think that bad boy deserves to be slapped hard?"

"Oh *yes*," said Bessie. "He does. Poor cat. I'll dry it a bit."

She got out her hanky and tried to dry the cat. But it was too wet.

"Don't trouble," said Johnny Stout, giving Johnny Thin a last hard slap that sent him off howling loudly. "I'll take the cat to Polly Flinders. She's always got a fire, and warms her pretty little toes by it!"

He picked up the cat and went into a nearby cottage. The children went and peeped in at the open door. They saw a little girl in the room inside, sitting close to a roaring fire, her toes wriggling in the heat.

Johnny Stout gave the cat to the little girl. "Here you are, Polly," he said. "Dry her a bit, will you? She got put down the well again. But I've given Johnny Thin a good slapping, so maybe he'll not do it any more."

Polly Flinders took the cat on her lap, making her pretty frock all wet. Johnny Stout was just going out of the door when somebody else came in. It was Polly Flinders' mother. When she saw Polly sitting among the cinders, warming her toes and nursing the wet cat, she gave a cry of rage.

"You naughty little girl! How many times have I told you not to sit so close to the fire? What's the good of dressing you up in nice clothes if you make them so dirty? I shall whip you!"

The children, Moon-Face and Watzisname felt rather scared of the cross mother. Johnny Stout ran away and the others thought it would be better to go too.

They went down the other side of the hill.

"Hallo!—who are these two coming up the hill?" said Moon-Face.

"Jack and Jill, of course!" said Bessie. And so they were, carrying a pail between them. They filled it at the well that stood at the top of the hill, and then began to go carefully down the hill.

"Oh—I do so hope they don't fall down," said Fanny, anxiously. "They always do, in the rhyme!"

Jack and Jill began to quarrel as they went down the hill. "Don't go so fast, Jack!" shouted Jill.

"You're always so slow!" grumbled Jack. "Do come on!"

"The pail's so heavy!" cried Jill, and began to lag behind just as they came to a steep bit.

"They'll fall down—and Jack will break his crown again—hurt his head badly!" said Bessie. "I'm going to stop them!"

She ran to the two children, who stopped, surprised. "Don't quarrel, Jack and Jill," begged Bessie. "You know you'll only fall down and hurt yourselves. Jill, let me take the handle of the pail. I can go as fast as Jack likes. Then for once in a way you will get to the bottom of the hill in safety, without falling down."

Jill let go the pail handle. Bessie took it. Jack

beamed at her. "Thank you," he said. "Jill's always so slow. Come along with me, and I'll give you one of my humbugs. I've got a whole bag full at home."

Bessie liked humbugs, with their brown and yellow stripes. "Oh, thank you," she said. "I'd like one." She turned to the others. "You go on to Miss Muffet's," she said. "I'll join you later."

So off went the others, whilst Jack, Jill and Bessie went down the hill together.

The others came to a gate on which was painted a name. "LITTLE MISS MUFFET".

"This is the place," said Jo, pleased. "Now we'll find old Saucepan. Hi, Saucepan, are you anywhere about?"

The door was shut. No one came. Jo banged on the knocker. Rat-a-tat-tat! Still no one came.

"There's someone peeping out of the window," said Moon-Face, suddenly. "It looks like Miss Muffet."

A little bit of curtain had been pushed to one side, and a frightened eye, a little nose, and a curl could be seen. That was all.

"It *is* Miss Muffet!" said Watzisname. "Miss Muffet, what's the matter? Why don't you open the door? Where is Saucepan?"

The curtain fell. There came a scamper of feet, and then the door opened just a crack. "Come in, quickly, all of you—quick, quick, quick!"

Her voice was so scared that it made everyone feel quite frightened. They crowded into the cottage quickly.

"What's the matter?" asked Moon-Face. "Has anything happened? Where's Saucepan? Didn't he come?"

"Yes, he came. But he was rude to my Spider," said Miss Muffet. "He danced all round it, clashing his kettles and saucepans, and he sang a rude song, that began 'Two smacks for a spider . . .'"

"Just like Saucepan!" groaned Moon-Face. "Well, what happened?"

"The spider pounced on him and carried him off," wept Miss Muffet. "I ordered him all the curds and whey in the house, but it didn't make any difference. He took no notice, and carried Saucepan away to his home. It's a sort of cave in the ground, with a door of web. No one can get through it except the spider."

"*Well!*" said Moon-Face, sitting down hard on a little chair. "How very annoying! How are we going to get him out? Why must he go and annoy the spider like that?"

"Well, the spider came and suddenly sat down beside me, and made me jump," said Miss Muffet. "He's always doing that. It made me run away, and Saucepan said he would give the spider a fright to pay him out."

"So he made up one of his silly songs, and did his crashing, clanging dance!" said Jo. "What are we going to do? Do you think the spider will let Saucepan go?"

"Oh no—not till the Land of Nursery Rhyme moves on," said Miss Muffet. "He means to punish him well. I don't know if Saucepan will mind living here. He doesn't really belong, of course."

"He'd hate to live here always and never see any of us except when the Land of Nursery Rhyme happened to come to the top of the Faraway Tree," said Moon-Face. "We must go and talk to that spider. Come on, all of you!"

"Oh—must I come?" asked Connie.

"Yes—the more of us that go, the better," said Watzisname. "The spider may feel afraid when he sees so many people marching up! You come too, Miss Muffet."

So they all went, to face the spider in his webby cave. Connie and Miss Muffet walked hand-in-hand behind, ready to run! They were neither of them very brave.

"Bessie will wonder where we are," said Jo, remembering that she had gone off with Jack and Jill. "Never mind—we'll find her when we've rescued Saucepan."

They came to a kind of cave in the ground. A door of thick grey web closed it. From inside came a mournful voice:

"Two smacks for a spider,
Two slaps on his nose.
Two whacks on his ankles,
Hi-tiddley-toze!"

"That's Saucepan, singing his rude spider-song again," whispered Miss Muffet. "Oh—look out! There's the spider!"

10.

Miss Muffet's Spider

"There's the spider! Here he comes!" cried everyone.

And there the spider certainly was. He was very large, had eight eyes to see with, and eight hairy legs to walk with. He wore a blue and red scarf round his neck, and he sneezed as he came.

"Wish-oo! Wish-oo! Bother this cold! No sooner do I lose one cold than I get another!"

He suddenly saw the little company of six people, and he stared with all his eight eyes. "What do *you* want?" he said.

Moon-Face went forward boldly, looking far braver than he felt.

"We've come to tell you to set our friend free," he said. "Open that webby door at once and let him out. We know he's down there, because we can hear him singing."

Out floated Saucepan's voice. "Two smacks for a spider . . ."

"There! He's singing that rude song again!" said the spider, looking most annoyed. "No, I certainly shan't let him go. He wants a lesson."

"I tell you, you *must* let him go!" said Moon-Face. "He doesn't belong to your Land. He belongs to ours. He'll be most unhappy here."

"Serve him right," said the spider. "A wish-oo! A wish-oo! Bother this cold."

"I hope you get hundreds of colds!" said Moon-Face, crossly. "Are you going to let Saucepan free, or shall we slash that door into bits?"

"Try, if you like!" said the spider, taking out a big red handkerchief from somewhere. "You'll be sorry, that's all I can say."

"Anyone got a knife?" asked Moon-Face. Nobody had. So Moon-Face marched to a nearby hedge and cut out two or three stout sticks. He gave one to Jo, one to Watzisname, and another to Fanny. He could see that Connie and Miss Muffet wouldn't be much use, so he didn't give them a stick.

"Now—slash down the door!", cried Moon-Face. The spider didn't say anything, but a horrid smile came on its face. It sat down and watched.

Moon-Face ran to the webby door and slashed at it with his stick. Jo and Watzisname slashed too, and Fanny followed.

But the webby door stuck to their sticks, and wound itself all round them. They tried to get it off, but the web stuck to them too. Soon it was floating about in long threads fastening itself round their legs and arms.

The spider got up. Connie and Miss Muffet were frightened and ran off as fast as they could. They hid under a bush and watched. They saw the spider push Jo, Moon-Face, Fanny and Watzisname into a heap together, and then roll them up in grey web so that they were caught like flies.

Then he bundled them all into his cave, and sat down to spin another webby door.

"A wish-oo!" sneezed the spider, suddenly. Then he coughed. He certainly had a terrible cold. He spied Connie and Miss Muffet under the bush and called to them.

"You come over here too, and I'll wrap you up nice and cosy in my web!"

Both Connie and Miss Muffet gave a squeal and ran back to Miss Muffet's cottage as fast as ever they could. When they got there they saw Bessie coming along with Jack and Jill.

"Hullo, Miss Muffet!" called Jack. "Fancy, because of Bessie's help, I got down the hill for the first time without falling over and hurting my head. Mother was very pleased, and she's given me a whole day off and Jill too. So we thought we'd come and spend it with the other children, and Moon-Face. Where are they?"

"Oh, they've been taken prisoner by Miss Muffet's spider!" said Connie. She told them all about it, and Bessie stared in dismay. What! Jo and Fanny being kept prisoner by a horrid old spider! Whatever could be done?

"And he had an awful cold," finished Connie. "I never knew spiders could catch colds before. He was coughing and sneezing just like we do."

"Sounds as if he ought to be in bed," said Jill. "Look out—here he comes!"

"A wish-oo!" said the spider, as he came by. "A wish-oo! Bother this cold!"

"Why don't you do something for it?" said Jill, stepping boldly forward. She knew the spider quite well, and was not afraid of him.

"Well, I've put a scarf on, haven't I?" said the spider, sniffing. "What more can I do?"

"You'd better put your feet in a mustard bath," said Jack. "That's what Mother makes us do if we have a bad cold. And we have to go to bed too, and drink hot lemon."

"That does sound nice and comforting," said the spider. "But I've got no bed, and no one to look after me—and no lemon."

"If Miss Muffet will lend you a bed, and squeeze you a lemon, Jack and I will look after you," said Jill. Miss Muffet stared at her in horror, but Jill gave her a nudge. She had a reason for saying all this. Miss Muffet swallowed hard and then nodded.

"All right! He can have my spare-room bed—but he is not to wander about my house and eat my curds and whey."

"I won't, I promise I won't," said the spider, gratefully. "I'll be very good indeed. Thank you, Miss Muffet. Perhaps I won't frighten you any more after this!"

"What about a bath to put his feet in?" said Jill. "You haven't a big enough one, Miss Muffet. You see, a spider has eight feet, not two."

"I've got a big bath in my cave," said the spider. "I'll go and get it."

"Certainly not," said Jack. "You mustn't go about in the open air any more, with that dreadful cold. You get into bed at once. *I'll* fetch your bath."

"But—but—there's a webby door over my cave—and you can't possibly get through it—and besides, there are prisoners there," said the spider.

"Well, tell me how to undo the door without getting caught up in that nasty webby stuff," said Jack. "Then I can get your bath and bring it."

"Have you got a nice big cotton-reel, Miss Muffet?" asked the spider. "You have? Good! Give it to Jack and he can take it with him. You'll find the end of the web-thread just by the handle of the webby door, Jack. Take hold of it and pull. Wind it round the reel and the web will all unravel nicely. You will be able to pull the door undone just like people pull a woollen jersey undone!"

"Well, I never!" said Jill, in surprise. "That's something to know, anyway. Is that the reel, Miss Muffet? Right! We'll go. We'll leave you to see the spider into bed, and squeeze him a lemon, and put a kettle on to boil. Then, when we come back with the bath, we can put mustard into a hot bath of water, and make the spider put his feet into it. Then his cold will soon be better."

The spider looked very happy at being cared for like this. He looked gratefully at the children out of his eight eyes.

Connie, Jack and Jill and Bessie set off. The spider called after them. "Hi! What about my prisoners? I don't want them to escape. You'll find them all bound up in web. Leave them like that, and put a stone or something over the mouth of my cave, will you?"

"We'll find a nice big stone," promised Jack. "Now hurry up and get into bed."

Soon the four of them got to the spider's cave and saw the webby door. Behind it they could hear Moon-Face groaning and grumbling, and Saucepan humming one of his songs.

"Look—there's the end of the web, sticking out just there!" said Connie, pointing to the middle of the door.

"Who's there?" called Jo, from below.

"Me, Connie," said Connie, "and Bessie too, and Jack and Jill, come to rescue you. We're going to undo the door."

Jack pulled at the web-end, and a thread

unravelled from the webby door. He wound it round and round the reel. Soon the door began to fall to pieces as all the thread it was made of was wound round the big cotton-reel. Then the children could see inside the cave. They saw Moon-Face, Watzisname, Saucepan, Jo and Fanny all in a heap together, bound tightly by the sticky spider-thread.

They went into the cave, but Jo called out to them in warning: "Don't come near us or you'll be all messed up in this horrid sticky web."

"I'm just going to find the end of the web that is binding you so tightly, and unravel it," said Jack. "Then you'll be free."

He found the end of the thread, and soon he was unravelling it like wool, and the four prisoners rolled over and over on the floor as their bonds were pulled away. And at last they were free!

"Oooh! Thank you," said Jo, sitting up. "I feel better now that sticky stuff is off. What a lot you've got on that cotton-reel, Jack!"

"Perhaps you would like to take it home and give it to Silky, as a little present," said Jack. "I know she often makes dresses, doesn't she?"

"Oh yes, she'd love it," said Jo, taking it. "Come on — let's get out of here and go home. I'm tired of Nursery Rhyme Land."

"We promised the spider we'd block up the door of his cave so that you couldn't escape," said Jack, with a grin. "You get out first, and we'll put a stone here after!"

So they did. Then, taking the spider's big bath on his shoulder, Jack led the way back. "Don't go near the window in case the spider sees you," he said to Moon-Face and the others. "I'll just fetch little Miss Muffet out to say good-bye to you, then you can go."

He went in with the bath. Miss Muffet had the kettle boiling and poured the water into it, adding a packet of yellow mustard. She stirred it up and called to the spider: "Come along—it's ready!"

He got out of bed and put his feet into it, all eight of them. Then he suddenly looked up. "I can hear my prisoners whispering together!" he said. "They must have escaped. I must go after them!"

II.

Back at Moon-Face's

Miss Muffet rushed to the door to warn the others to go. "He's heard you whispering together!" she said. "Go quickly!"

The children and the others all fled, Jack and Jill too. The spider took his feet out of the hot mustard bath and looked round for a towel to dry them.

"I shan't give you a towel," said Miss Muffet, severely. "You can go after them with wet feet, and get an even worse cold, and be dreadfully ill. But I won't nurse you then."

The spider sneezed. "A-wish-oo, a-wish-oo! Oh dear, this is really a dreadful cold. I don't want to make it any worse. I'll be good and put my feet back. I'll have to let my prisoners escape."

"There's a good spider," said Miss Muffet.

He was pleased. "I wish I could have a hot water bottle, Miss Muffet. I've never had one."

"Well, as you've let your prisoners go, I'll lend you my bottle," said Miss Muffet, and went to get it.

Jo, Moon-Face, Saucepan and the others had by this time got to the top of the hill and down the other side. They looked back but could see no sign of the spider.

"He's not coming after us, after all," said Bessie thankfully. "Where's the hole through the cloud?"

"We'll show you," said Jack and Jill. "We'd rather like to come down it with you, and see the Faraway Tree."

"Oh *do*!" said everyone. "Come and have some dinner with us."

"I'll send down to Silky and get her to come up and help to make some sandwiches," said Moon-Face.

When they came to the hole in the cloud they all slid down the ladder and branch, and went to Moon-Face's house. Jack and Jill were amused to see his curved furniture.

They sent the red squirrel down to fetch Silky. She had been out shopping all morning, and came up delighted to know that Jo and the others were up the tree. She squealed with delight to see Jack and Jill too.

"Hallo!" she cried. "It's ages since I saw you two. Do you still fall down the hill? Jack, you haven't got your head done up in vinegar and brown paper, for a wonder!"

"No—because Bessie kindly helped me carry the pail of water down the hill to-day," said Jack. "And she goes faster than Jill, so we didn't fall over through getting out of step. We've had a lot of adventures to-day, Silky."

"Oh, Silky, here's a present for you," said Jo, remembering, and he gave the pretty little elf the cotton-reel on which he had wound the spider-thread.

"Oh thank you, Jo!" cried Silky. "Just what I want! I couldn't get any fine thread at all this morning. This will do beautifully."

"Will you help to make some sandwiches, Silky?" said Moon-Face. "We thought we'd have a picnic dinner up here. Let me see—how many are there of us?"

"Six children—and four others," counted Jo. "Ten. You'll have to make about a hundred sandwiches!"

"It's a pity the Land of Goodies isn't here," said Moon-Face. "We could go up and take what food we wanted then and bring it down. Got any Google Buns or Pop Biscuits, Silky dear?"

"I've got some Pop Biscuits in my basket somewhere," said Silky. "Do Jack and Jill know them?"

They didn't, and they did enjoy them. They went pop as soon as they were put into the mouth, and honey flowed out from the middle of each biscuit!

"Delicious!" said Jack. "I could do with a few dozen of these biscuits."

Soon they were all sitting on the broad branch outside Moon-Face's house, eating sandwiches and biscuits and drinking lemonade.

There was as much lemonade as anyone liked, because, in a most friendly manner, the Faraway Tree suddenly began to grow ripe yellow lemons on the branches round about. All Moon-Face had to do was pick them, cut them in half, and squeeze them into a jug. Then he added water and sugar, and the children drank the lemonade!

"This is a marvellous Tree," said Connie, leaning back happily. "Simply marvellous. You *are* clever, Moon-Face, to make such lovely lemonade."

"Dear me. Connie seems to be believing in the Tree at last," said Jo. "Do you, Connie?"

"Yes, I do," said Connie. "I can't help it. I didn't like that spider adventure—but this is lovely, sitting here and eating these delicious sandwiches and Pop Biscuits, and drinking lemonade from lemons growing on the Tree."

She shook the branch she was leaning on, and some ripe lemons fell off. They went bumping down the tree.

There came a yell from below.

"Now then! Who's throwing ripe lemons at me, I should like to know. One's got in my wash-tub. Any more of that and I'll come up and spank the thrower."

"There!" said Moon-Face to Connie. "See what

you've done! Shaken down heaps of juicy lemons on to Dame Washalot. She'll be after you if you're not careful."

"Oooh!" said Connie, in alarm. She called down the tree. "I'm so sorry, Dame Washalot. It was quite an accident."

"Connie's getting some manners," said Jo to Bessie. "Any more Pop Biscuits? Have another, Saucepan?"

"Mother's very well, thank you," said Saucepan.

"I said 'Have ANOTHER'?" said Jo.

"You haven't asked him to sell you a saucepan," said Bessie. "Ask him about a saucepan for Mother."

"Have you got a saucepan that would do for our mother?" asked Jo. "I want a nice little saucepan to boil milk."

"Oiled silk?" said Saucepan. "No, my mother doesn't wear oiled silk. Why should she? She wears black, with a red shawl and a red belt and a bonnet with . . ."

"Can't we get away from Saucepan's mother?" groaned Jo. "I never even knew he had one. I wonder where she lives."

Saucepan unexpectedly heard this. "She lives in the Land of Dame Slap," he said. "She's her cook. She needs lots of saucepans because she has to cook meals for all the children at her school."

"Gracious!" said Bessie, remembering. "We've been to Dame Slap's Land! We flew there once in an aeroplane. We had an awful time because Dame Slap put us into her school!"

"Does your mother really live there?" said Jo
"Do you ever go to see her?"

"Oh yes, when I can," said Saucepan. "I believe
Dame Slap's Land is coming next week. I'd like
you all to meet my dear old mother. She will give
you a most wonderful tea."

There was a silence. No one wanted to be mixed
up with Dame Slap again. She was a most
unpleasant person.

"*Well?*" said Saucepan, looking round. "I
didn't hear anyone say 'Thank you very much,
we'd love to know your mother'."

"Well, you see—er—er—it's a bit awkward,"
said Moon-Face. "You see, your mother being
cook to Dame Slap—er . . ."

"I suppose you are trying to say that my dear
old mother isn't good enough for you to meet!"
said Saucepan, unexpectedly, and looked terribly
hurt and cross. "All right. If you won't know my
mother, you shan't know *me!*"

And to everyone's alarm he got up and walked
straight up the branch into the cloud, and
disappeared into the Land of Nursery Rhyme.
Everyone yelled after him.

"Saucepan, we'd love to meet your mother, but
we don't like Dame Slap!"

"Saucepan, come BACK!"

But Saucepan either didn't or wouldn't hear.
"You go and fetch him back," said Jo to Jack and
Jill. So up they went after him. But they soon
came back.

"Can't see him anywhere," they said. "He isn't

to be found. I expect he is hiding himself away in a temper. He'll soon be back again."

But Saucepan didn't come back.

"We'll have to go home," said Jo, at last. "Let us know when Saucepan comes back, Moon-Face. Tell him we would love to meet his old mother, and it's all a mistake. All the same—I hope he *won't* want us to go to Dame Slap's Land —I shouldn't like that at all."

"Go down the Slippery-Slip," said Moon-Face, throwing the children cushions. "Yes, I feel upset about Saucepan too. He isn't usually so touchy. You go first, Jo."

Jo sat on his cushion, gave himself a push and down he went, whizzing round and round the Slippery-Slip right to the bottom of the Tree.

He shot out of the trap-door and landed on the tuft of moss. He got up hurriedly, knowing that Connie was coming down just behind him.

Soon all four were at the foot of the Tree. The squirrel collected the cushions and disappeared with them. Jo linked arms with the girls, and they turned towards home.

"Well, that was quite an adventure," Jo said. "I guess you don't want to meet Miss Muffet's spider again, Connie?"

"No, I don't," said Connie. "But I'd like to please old Saucepan, and meet his mother, even if he hasn't been very nice to me so far."

"You're getting quite a nice little girl, Connie!" said Jo, in surprise. "Well—maybe we'll all have to go and meet his mother next week. We'll see!"

12.

Saucepan is Very Cross

For a few days the children did not hear anything from their friends in the Faraway Tree.

"I wonder if the old Saucepan Man calmed down a bit and went back to Moon-Face's," said Jo.

On the fifth or sixth day there came a knock at the door. Jo opened it. Outside was the red squirrel and he had a note in his paw.

"For you all," he said, and gave it to Jo. "There's an answer, please."

Jo slit the envelope and read the note out loud.

"DEAR EVERYBODY,

"When are you coming to see us again? Old Saucepan came back yesterday from the Land of Nursery Rhyme. He had been staying with Polly-Put-the-Kettle-On. He gave her a new kettle, and she said he could stay with her in return. He is still upset because he says we don't want to meet his dear old mother. He won't speak to any of us. He is living with the Owl, and he has made up a lot of rude songs about us. Will you come and see if you can put things right? He might listen to you. He won't take any notice of me or Silky or Watzisname. So do come.

"Love from
"MOON-FACE."

"Well!" said Jo, putting the note back into its envelope. "Funny old Saucepan! Who would have thought he would be so touchy? Why, I'd love to meet his mother. She must be a dear old thing."

"It's only that she's Dame Slap's cook and if we go and see her, Dame Slap might catch us again," said Bessie. "We had an awful time with her last time."

"We'd better go up the Tree to-morrow, and tell Saucepan exactly what we think, and make sure he hears and understands us," said Fanny. "Let's do that."

"Is that the answer then?" asked the red squirrel, politely.

"Yes, that's the answer," said Jo. "We'll be up the Tree to-morrow—and we'll try and put things right. Tell Moon-Face that."

The squirrel bounded off. The children looked after him. "What a dependable little fellow that squirrel is," said Jo. "Well—we must go up the Tree tomorrow, no doubt about that. Coming, too, Connie?"

"Oh yes," said Connie, beginning to feel excited again. "Of course. I'd love to, Jo."

So the next day off to the Faraway Tree went the four children. "We'll climb up," said Jo. "Because if Saucepan is living in the Owl's home, it's only just a little way past the Angry Pixie's, and we can call for him there."

So, when they came to the Tree, they didn't send for cushions to go up on, but began to climb.

The Tree was growing black-currants, ripe and juicy. It was fun to pick them, and bite into them feeling the rich, sweet juice squirt out.

All of them had black mouths as they climbed. They came to the Angry Pixie's, and Connie kept well away from the window this time. But his door was open, and he was out. A small field-mouse was busy scrubbing the floor, and another one was shaking the mats.

"Bit of spring-cleaning going on," said Jo, as they passed. "I suppose the Angry Pixie's gone out for the day, to get away from it!"

Soon they came to the Owl's home. They peeped cautiously in at the window. Saucepan was there, polishing his kettles at top speed, making them shine brightly. He was singing one of his silly songs, very loudly:

"Two spankings for Connie,
Two smackings for Jo,
Two scoldings for Bessie,
Hi-tiddly-ho!"

"Two drubbings for Moon-Face,
Two snubbings for Fan,
Two slappings for Silky,
From the old Saucepan Man!"

"Gracious! He must still be in a very bad temper," said Bessie, quite hurt. "And fancy talking about slapping Silky. He's always been so fond of her."

88

"Do you think we'd better stop and talk to him now or not?" said Jo.

"Not," said Fanny at once. "He'll only be rude and horrid. Let's go up to Moon-Face and Silky, and see what they suggest."

So up the Tree they went, leaving behind the cross old Saucepan Man, still polishing his kettles hard. They just dodged Dame Washalot's water in time. They heard it coming and darted to the other side of the tree. They waited till it had all gone down, then climbed up again.

They came to Silky's house and knocked at the door. Moon-Face opened it, and beamed.

"Hallo! So you've come all right! Come along in. I was just having a cup of cocoa with Silky."

They all crowded into Silky's dear little tree-house and sat down. Silky poured them out cups of cocoa, and handed round some new Pop biscuits. How Connie loved the pop they made, and the honey that flowed out from the middle! She sat enjoying her lunch and listened to the others talking.

"Saucepan is really awful," said Silky. "He sings rude songs about us all day long, and all the Tree-Folk laugh!"

"Yes. We heard the songs," said Jo. "Not very kind of him, is it? What can we do about it? Will he listen to us, do you think, if we go back and talk nicely to him?"

"I don't know," said Moon-Face, doubtfully. "When Silky and I went down to him last night to beg him to be sensible and to be friends, he sang his songs at us, and did his clashing, clanging dance. He frightened everyone in the Tree, and Dame Washalot sent a message to say that if the noise went on she would empty twenty wash-tubs down at once, and drown us all!"

"We can't let Saucepan go on like this," said Bessie. "How can we put him into a good temper, and make him ashamed of himself?"

"I know!" said Connie, unexpectedly. "Let's go down and take presents from us to his mother. Then he will be so pleased he will be nice again."

Everyone stared at Connie. "Well, if that isn't a splendid idea!" said Silky. "Why didn't we think of it before? Saucepan will be thrilled!"

"Yes, really, Connie, that's a fine idea!" said Bessie, and Connie went red with pleasure. The others ticked her off so much that it was very pleasant to be praised for a change.

"Connie's getting quite nice," Fanny said to Silky and Moon-Face. "Now she's not an only child, but has to live with us, she's different— not so silly and selfish. You'll get to like her soon."

"It's a good idea, to take presents to Saucepan for his mother," said Moon-Face. "We'll do that. It's the one thing that will make him smile and beam. What shall we take?"

"I'll look in my treasure-bag," said Silky, "and you go up to your house and see if you've anything that would please an old lady, Moon-Face."

Moon-Face went off. The others watched as Silky turned out what she called her "treasure-bag." It had lots of pretty things in it.

"Here's a lovely set of buttons," said Silky, picking up a set of three red buttons, made like poppy-heads. "She'd like those."

"And what about this pink rose for a bonnet?" said Bessie, picking up a rose that looked so real she felt sure it must have a smell. It had! "This would do beautifully for an old lady."

"And here's a hat-pin with a little rabbit sitting at one end," said Fanny. "She'd like that."

Just then Moon-Face came back. He brought with him three things—a tiny vase for flowers, a brooch with M. on it for Mother, and a shoe-horn made of silver. The others thought they would be lovely for the old lady.

"We can each take one and give it to Saucepan for his mother," said Moon-Face. "Come on! We'll let Silky do the talking. Saucepan is fondest of her. Don't let him see you at first, Connie. He doesn't like you."

They all went down to the Owl's home. They peeped inside. Saucepan had finished polishing his kettles, and was sitting quite silent, looking gloomy.

"Go on, Silky!" whispered Moon-Face. So Silky went in first, holding out the pink rose.

"Dear Saucepan, I've brought you a present to give to your mother from me, when you see her," she said, in her very loudest voice. For a wonder Saucepan heard every word. He looked at Silky, and said nothing at first. Then he said:

"For my old mother? Oh, how kind of you,

Silky! She'll love this pink rose."

"Quick, come on!" whispered Moon-Face to the others. So they all crowded in, holding out their gifts nervously, and saying, "For your mother, Saucepan."

Saucepan put each gift solemnly into one of his kettles or saucepans. He seemed very touched.

"Thank you," he said. "Thank you very much. My mother will be delighted. It's her birthday soon. I will take her these presents from you. I expect she will invite you to her birthday party."

"That would be very nice," said Jo, in a loud voice. "But Saucepan, we don't like Dame Slap, and you said your mother was her cook. If we go to see her, will you promise we don't get put into Dame Slap's school again? We went there once and she was horrid to us."

"Oh, of course I'll see to that," said the old Saucepan Man, who looked quite his old cheery self again. "I'm sorry I sang rude songs about you. It was all a mistake. I'll go up into Dame Slap's Land to-morrow and see my dear old mother, and take your gifts and messages. Then you can come and have tea with her on her birthday."

"All right!" said Jo. "We'd like to do that—but mind, Saucepan, we don't want even to see Dame Slap in the distance."

"You shan't," said Saucepan.

But oh dear—they did!

13.

In the Land of Dame Slap

It wasn't very long before a message came from Moon-Face. "I have heard from Saucepan. He says we are to go up to Dame Slap's Land to-morrow, and have tea. If we go to the back door of the school, his mother will be there."

So the next day, the four children set off. They went up the Faraway Tree, and called for Silky first. She had on a pretty party frock, and had washed her hair, which was more like a golden mist than ever.

"I'm just ready," she said, giving her hair a last brush. "I hope Moon-Face won't keep us waiting. He had lost his hat this morning, and he's been rushing up and down the tree all day, asking everyone if they've seen it."

When they got to Moon-Face's he was quite ready, beaming as usual, a floppy hat on his head.

"Oh, you found your hat then," said Silky.

"Yes — it had fallen down the Slippery-Slip," said Moon-Face. "And when I went down there, I shot out of the trap-door at the bottom, and there was my hat on my feet! So that was all right. Are we all ready?"

"Yes," said Jo. "But do for goodness' sake look out for Dame Slap. I really do feel nervous of her."

"Saucepan will be looking out for us, don't worry," said Moon-Face. "I expect he will be at the top of the ladder, waiting. We are sure to have a lovely tea. His mother is a most marvellous cook."

They climbed up the topmost branch of the Tree, and came to the ladder. They all went up it and found themselves in Dame Slap's Land. There wasn't much to see – only, in the distance, a large green house set in the middle of a great garden.

"That's Dame Slap's school," said Jo to Connie.

"Who goes to it?" asked Connie, curiously.

"All the bad pixies and fairies and brownies," said Bessie. "We saw some once when we were there. Dame Slap has to be very stern or she wouldn't be able to teach them. They are very naughty."

"Where's the back-door?" said Connie, looking nervously round. "Let's go there, quick. I do think Saucepan might have waited for us at the top of the ladder."

"Yes, I don't know why he didn't," said Moon-Face, rather puzzled. "Shall we call him?"

"No, of course not, silly," said Jo. "We'll have Dame Slap after us at once! Come on – we'll find the back-door. We really can't wait about any longer."

So they went round the large garden, keeping carefully outside the tall wall, until they came to two gates. One opened on to the drive that led to the front door. The other opened on to a path that plainly led to the back-door.

"This is where we go," said Bessie, and they went quietly through the back gate. They came to the back-door. It was shut. No one seemed to be about.

"I suppose Saucepan and his mother *are* expecting us?" said Jo, puzzled. He knocked on the door. There was no answer. He knocked again.

"Let's open the door and go in," said Bessie, impatiently. "We must find Saucepan. I expect he's forgotten he asked us to come to-day."

They pushed open the door and went into a big and very tidy kitchen. There was no one there. It seemed very strange. Connie opened the further door and peered into what seemed to be a big hall.

"I believe I can hear someone," she said. "I'll go and see if it's Saucepan."

Before the others could stop her she had opened the door and gone. No one felt that they wanted to follow. They sat down in the kitchen and waited.

Connie went into the big hall. There was no one there. She went into another room, that looked like a drawing-room. Connie peered round it in curiosity. Then, in at a door opposite came a tall old woman, with large spectacles on her long nose and a big white bonnet on her head.

"Oh!" said Connie, beaming. "Many happy returns of the day! Where's Saucepan? We've all come to have tea with you?"

The old woman stopped in surprise. "Indeed!" she said. "You have, have you? And who are the rest of you?"

"Oh—didn't Saucepan tell you?" asked Connie. "There's Jo and Bessie and Fanny and Moon-

Face and Silky. We did hope that Saucepan would meet us by the ladder, because we were so afraid of meeting that awful Dame Slap."

"Oh, really?" said the old woman, and her eyes gleamed behind her big spectacles. "You think she's awful, do you?"

"Well, Jo and the others told me all about her," said Connie. "They were all here once, you know, and they escaped. They were very much afraid of meeting her again."

"Where are they?" said the old woman.

"In the kitchen," said Connie. "I'll go and tell them I've found you."

She ran ahead of the old woman, who followed her at once. Connie flung open the kitchen door.

"I've found Saucepan's mother!" she said. "Here she is!"

The old lady came into the room—and Jo and the others gave a gasp of horror. It wasn't Saucepan's mother. It was Dame Slap herself, looking simply furious.

"Dame Slap!" yelled Jo. "Run, everyone!"

But it was too late. Dame Slap turned the key in the kitchen door and put it into her pocket.

"So you escaped from me before, did you?" she said. "Well, you won't escape again. Bad children who are sent to me to be made good don't usually escape before they are taught the things they ought to know!"

"Look here!" began Moon-Face, putting a bold face on. "Look here, Dame Slap, we didn't come to see you; we came to see Saucepan's mother."

"I've never in my life heard of Saucepan," said Dame Slap. "Never. It's a naughty story. You're making it up. I slap people for telling stories."

And she gave poor Moon-Face such a slap that he yelled.

"Saucepan's mother is your cook!" he shouted, dodging round the kitchen. "Your cook! Where is she?"

"Oh—my cook," said Dame Slap. "Well, she walked out yesterday, along with a dreadful creature who was all hung round with kettles and pans."

"That was Saucepan," groaned Jo. "Where did they go?"

"I don't know and I certainly don't care," said Dame Slap. "The cook was most rude to me, and I gave her a good slap. So she went off. Can any of you girls cook?"

"I can," said Bessie. "But if you think I'm going to be your cook now, you're mistaken. I'm going home to my mother."

"You can stay here and cook for me till my old cook comes back," said Dame Slap. "And this girl can help you." She pointed to Fanny. "The others can come into my school and learn to work hard, to get good manners and to be well-behaved children. Go along now!"

To Jo's horror she pushed everyone but Bessie and Fanny into the hall, and up the stairs to a big classroom, where dozens of noisy little imps, fairies and pixies were playing and pushing and fighting together.

Dame Slap dealt out a few hard smacks and sent them to their seats, yelling.

Connie was very much afraid. She stayed close to Jo and Moon-Face. Dame Slap made them all sit down at the back of the room.

"Silence!" she said. "You will now do your homework. The new children will please find pencils and paper in their desks. Everyone must answer the questions on the board. If anyone gets them wrong, they will have to be punished."

"Oh dear!" groaned Silky. Connie whispered to her:

"Don't worry! I'm awfully good at lessons. I shall know all the answers, and I'll tell you them too."

"Who is whispering?" shouted Dame Slap, and everyone jumped. "You, new girl, come out here."

Connie came out, trembling. Dame Slap gave her a hard smack on each hand.

"Stop crying!" said Dame Slap. And Connie stopped. She gave a gulp, and stopped at once. "Go back to your seat and do your homework," ordered the old dame. So back Connie went.

"Now, no talking and no playing," said Dame Slap. "Just hard work. I am going to talk to my new cooks in the kitchen about a Nice Treacle Pudding. If I hear anyone talking or playing when I come back, or if anyone hasn't done the homework, there will be no Nice Treacle Pudding for any of you."

With this awful threat Dame Slap walked out of the room. She left the door wide open so that she could hear any noise.

The imp in front of Connie turned round and shook his pen on her book. A big blot came there! The goblin next to him pulled Silky's hair. A bright-eyed pixie threw a rubber at Moon-Face and hit him on the nose. Truly Dame Slap's pupils were a mischievous lot!

"We *must* do our homework!" whispered Silky to the others. "Connie, read the questions on the board, and tell us the answers, quick!"

So Connie read them—but, oh, dear me, how could she answer questions like that? She never, never could. They would all go without pudding, and be slapped and sent to bed! Oh dear, oh dear, oh dear!

14.

Dame Slap's School

The more the children looked at the three questions on the board, the more they felt certain they could never answer them. Moon-Face turned to Connie. "Quick! Tell us the right answers. You said you were good at lessons."

Connie read the first question. "Three blackbirds sat on a cherry tree. They ate one hundred and twenty-three of the cherries. How many were left?"

"Well, how can we say, unless we know how many there were in the beginning?" said Connie, out loud. "What a silly question!"

Jo read the next one out loud. "If there are a hundred pages in a book, how many books would there be on the shelf?"

"The questions are just nonsense," said Moon-Face, gloomily.

"They were before, when we were here," said Jo.

The third question was very short. Jo read it out. "Why is a blackboard?"

"Why is a blackboard!" repeated Silky. "There is no sense in that question either."

"Well—the questions are nonsense, so we'll put down answers that are nonsense," said Jo.

So they put down "none" about how many cherries were left on the tree. Then they read the book-question again. And again they put down "none".

"We are not told that the shelf was a book-shelf," said Jo. "It might be a shelf for ornaments, or a bathroom shelf for glasses and tooth-brushes and things. There wouldn't be any books there."

The third question was a puzzler. "Why is a blackboard?"

Jo ran out of his place and rubbed out the two last words. He wrote them again—and then the question read "Why is a board black?"

"We can easily answer that," said Jo, with a grin. "Why is a board black? So that we can write on it with white chalk!"

So, when Dame Slap came back, the only
people who had answered all the questions were
Jo, Silky, Moon-Face and Connie! Dame Slap
beamed at them.

"Dear me, I have some clever children at last!"
she said. "You have written answers to all the
questions."

"Then they are right?" asked Silky, in wonder.

"I don't know," said Dame Slap. "But that
doesn't matter. It's the answers I want. I don't
care what's in them, so long as you have written
answers. I don't know the answers myself, so it's
no good my reading them."

Then Moon-Face undid all the good they had

done by giving an extremely rude snort. "Pooh! What a silly school this is! Fancy giving people questions if you don't know the answers! Pooh!"

"Don't 'pooh' at me like that!" said Dame Slap, getting angry all of a sudden. "Go to bed! Off to bed with you for the rest of the day!"

"But—but," began poor Moon-Face, in alarm, wishing he had not spoken, "but . . ."

"You'll turn into a goat in a minute, if you are so full of 'buts'," said Dame Slap, and she pushed Moon-Face out of the door. She drove the others out too, and took them to a small bedroom, in which were four tiny beds, very hard and narrow.

"Now, into bed you get, and nothing but bread and water for you all day long. I will not have rudeness in my school!"

She shut the door and locked it. Moon-Face looked at the others in dismay. "I'm sorry I made her do this," he said. "Very sorry. But really, she did make me feel so cross. Do you think we'd better go to bed? She might smack us hard if we don't."

Connie leapt into bed at once, fully dressed as she was. She wasn't going to risk Dame Slap coming back and slapping her! The others did the same. They drew the sheets up to their chins and lay there gloomily. This was a horrid adventure—just when they had so much looked forward to coming out to tea too.

"I wonder what Bessie and Fanny are doing," said Moon-Face. "Cooking hard, I suppose. I do think Saucepan might have warned us that his mother had gone. It's too bad."

Just then there came the sound of a song floating up from outside.

"Two worms for a sparrow,
Two slugs for a duck,
Two snails for a blackbird,
Two hens for a cluck!"

"Saucepan! It must be Saucepan!" cried everyone, and jumped out of bed and ran to the window. Outside, far down below, stood Saucepan, and with him were Bessie and Fanny, giggling.

"Hi, Saucepan! Here we are!" cried Jo. "We're locked in."

"Oh—we wondered where you were," said Saucepan, grinning. "Dame Slap's locked in, too —locked into the larder by sharp young Bessie here. She was just doing it when I came along to see if you had arrived."

"Arrived! We've been here ages," said Jo, indignantly. "Why didn't you come to warn us?"

"My watch must be wrong again," said Saucepan. He usually kept it in one of his kettles, but as it shook about there every day, it wasn't a very good time-keeper. "Never mind. I'll rescue you now."

A terrific banging noise came from somewhere downstairs. "That's Dame Slap in the larder," said Saucepan. "She's in a dreadful temper."

"Well, for goodness' sake, help us out of here," said Connie, alarmed. "How can we get out? The door's locked, and I heard Dame Slap taking the key out the other side."

Crash! Bang! Clatter!

"Sounds as if Dame Slap is throwing a few pies and things about," said Jo. "Saucepan, how can we get out of here?"

"I'll just undo the rope that hangs my things round me," said Saucepan, and he began to untie the rope round his waist. He undid it, and then, to the children's surprise, his kettles and saucepans began to peel off him. They were each tied firmly to the rope.

"Saucepan does look funny without his kettles and pans round him," said Connie in surprise. "I hardly know him!"

Saucepan took the end of the rope and tied a stone to it. He threw it up to the window. Jo caught the stone and pulled on the rope. It came up, laden here and there with kettles and saucepans.

"Tie the rope-end to a bed," called Saucepan. "Then come down the rope. You can use the kettles and saucepans as steps. They are tied on quite tightly."

So, very cautiously, Moon-Face, Jo, Silky and a very nervous Connie climbed down the rope, using the saucepans and kettles as steps. They were very glad to stand on firm ground again!

"Well, there we are," said Saucepan, pleased. "Wasn't that a good idea?"

"Yes—but how are we to get your stock of kettles and saucepans back for you?" said Jo.

"It doesn't matter at all," said Saucepan. "I can take as many as I can carry out of the kitchen here. They are what I gave my mother each birthday, you know, so they are hers."

He went into the kitchen and collected a great array of kettles and saucepans. He tied them all to a rope, and then once more became the old Saucepan Man they knew so well, hung around with pans of all shapes and sizes!

Crash! Smash! Clang! Dame Slap was getting angrier and angrier in the larder. She kicked and she stamped.

"Dame Slap!" cried Jo, suddenly, and he stood outside the locked larder door. "I will ask you a question, and if you can tell me the answer, I will set you free. Now, be quiet and listen."

There was a silence in the larder. Jo asked his question.

"If Saucepan takes twelve kettles from your kitchen, how long does it take to boil a cup of tea on Friday?"

The others giggled. There came an angry cry from the larder. "It's a silly question, and there's no answer. Let me out at once!"

"It's the same kind of question you asked *us*!" said Jo. "I'm sorry you can't answer it. I can't either. So you must stay where you are, till one of your school children is kind enough to let you out. Good-bye, dear Dame Slap!"

The children and the others went out giggling into the garden. "Where are we going now?" asked Bessie. "Where's your mother, Saucepan?"

"She's in the Land of Tea-Parties," said Saucepan. "It's not very far. I took her there because it's her birthday, you know, and I thought she'd like to have a tea-party without going to any trouble. Shall we go?"

So, hearing Dame Slap's furious cries and bangs gradually fading behind them, the little party set off together, very glad to have escaped from Dame Slap in safety.

"Come on—here's the boundary between this Land and the next. Jump!" said Saucepan.

They jumped—and over they went into the Land of Tea-Parties! What a fine time they meant to have there!

15.

The Land of Tea-Parties

The Land of Tea-Parties was peculiar. It seemed to be made up of nothing but white-clothed tables laden with all kinds of good things to eat!

"Gracious!" said Jo, looking round. "What a lot of tables—big and small, round and square—and all filled with the most gorgeous things to eat!"

"They've got chairs set round them too," said Fanny. "All ready for people to sit on."

"And look at the little waiters!" said Connie, in delight. "They are rabbits!"

So they were — rabbits dressed neatly in aprons, and little black coats, hurrying here and there, carrying pots of tea, jugs of lemonade, and all kinds of other drinks.

It was lovely to watch them; they were so very busy and so very serious.

"There are some people choosing tables already!" said Jo, pointing. "Look — that must be a pixie's tea-party, sitting over there. Aren't they sweet?"

"And oh, do look! — there's a squirrel party," said Fanny. "Mother and Father Squirrel, and all the baby squirrels. I expect it's one of the baby squirrels' birthdays!"

It was fun to see the little tea-parties. But soon the children began to feel very hungry. There were such nice things on the tables! There were sandwiches of all kinds, stuck with little labels to show what they were. Fanny read some of them out loud.

"Dewdrop and honey sandwiches — ooh! And here are some sardine and strawberry sandwiches — what a funny mixture! But I dare say it would be nice. And here are orange and lemon sandwiches — I've never heard of those. And pineapple and cucumber! Really, what an exciting lot of things!"

"Look at the cakes!" said Connie. "I've never seen such beauties."

Nor had anyone else. There were pink cakes, yellow cakes, chocolate cakes, ginger cakes, cakes with fruit and silver balls all over them, cakes with icing, cakes with flowers on made of sugar, cakes big as could be, and tiny ones only enough for two persons.

There were jellies and fruit salads and ice-creams too. Which table should they choose? There were different things at every table!

"Here's one with chocolate ice-cream," said Connie. "Let's have this one."

"No—I'd like this one—it's got blue jellies, and I've never seen those before," said Silky.

"Well, oughtn't we to find Saucepan's mother before we do anything?" said Moon-Face.

"Gracious, of course we ought!" said Bessie. "Seeing all these gorgeous things made me forget we had come to have tea with Saucepan's mother. SAUCEPAN, WHERE IS YOUR MOTHER?"

"Over there," said Saucepan, and he pointed to where the dearest little old woman stood waiting, her apple-cheeks rosy red, and her bright eyes twinkling as brightly as Saucepan's. "She's waiting. She's got the pink rose in her bonnet, look!—and the hat-pin—and she's sewn the red poppy buttons on her dress, and she's pinned the M for Mother brooch in front. The only thing she can't wear are the shoe-horn and the vase, and I think she's got them in her pocket. She was awfully pleased with everything."

"Let's go and wish her many happy returns of the day," said Bessie, so they all went over to the dear little old lady, and wished her a very happy birthday. She was delighted to see them all, and she kissed them, each one, even Moon-Face.

"Well, I *am* glad you've come," she said. "I

began to think something had happened to you."

"It had," said Jo, and he began to tell her about Dame Slap. But old Mrs. Saucepan was just as deaf as Saucepan himself was.

"Here you are at last," said Mrs. Saucepan to Saucepan.

"Yes, we did come fast," agreed Saucepan. "We locked Dame Slap in the larder."

"Harder?" said Mrs. Saucepan. "Harder than what?"

The children giggled. Jo went up to Mrs. Saucepan and spoke very clearly.

"Let's have tea! The tables are getting filled up!"

Mrs. Saucepan heard. "Yes, we will," she said.

"I'd like a table with blue jellies," said Silky.

"I'd like one with pineapple and cucumber sandwiches," said Connie.

"Well—as it's Saucepan's mother's birthday, don't you think we ought to let *her* choose the table?" said Bessie. "She ought to have the things *she* likes best to-day."

"Yes, of course," said the others, rather ashamed not to have thought of that. "MRS. SAUCEPAN, PLEASE CHOOSE YOUR OWN TABLE."

Well, Mrs. Saucepan went straight to a big round table, set with eight chairs, and sat down at the head of it—and wasn't it strange, there were blue jellies there for Silky, pineapple and cucumber sandwiches for Connie, a big fat chocolate cake for Moon-Face, and all the things the others wanted too!

"This is glorious," said Connie, beginning on the sandwiches. "Oh—I never in my life tasted such beautiful sandwiches, never!"

The little rabbit waiters ran up, and bowed to old Mrs. Saucepan. "What will you have to drink?" they asked.

"Tea for me," said Mrs. Saucepan. "What for you others?"

"Lemonade! Ginger-beer! Orange-ade! Lime-juice! Cherry-ade!" called the children and the others. The rabbits ran off, and came back with trays on which stood opened bottles of everything asked for, and a fat brown teapot of tea for Mrs. Saucepan.

What fun they all had! There were squeals of laughter from everyone, and from every table there came happy chattering. The Land of Tea-Parties was certainly a great success.

The children finished up with ice-cream. Then the rabbits brought round big gay boxes of crackers, and the air was soon full of pops and bangs. Mrs. Saucepan pulled crackers with each of them, and there were lovely things inside—brooches, and rings and little toys, and comical hats that everyone put on at once.

"Well, we've had a glorious time," said Jo, at last; "but I think we ought to go now, Mrs. Saucepan. Thank you very much for asking us here. I hope you get another job as cook some-where soon."

"Oh, I think I shall go and live in the Faraway Tree with Dame Washalot," said Mrs. Saucepan.

She's always so busy with her washing, she hasn't much time to cook. I could do the cooking for her. I could make cakes to sell too, and have a little shop there."

"Oh — that would be absolutely lovely!" cried Bessie. "I'll come and buy from you often."

"We'd better go back through the Land of Dame Slap very cautiously indeed," said Moon-Face. "We can't get back to the Tree from this Land because it's not over the Tree. We shall have to creep back through Dame Slap's Land and rush to the ladder quickly."

So they said good-bye to the busy little rabbit waiters, and jumped over the boundary line again, back into Dame Slap's Land. They had to pass near the school, of course, and they listened hard to see what was going on.

There was a most terrific noise of shouting, laughing and squealing. The grounds of the school were full of the school-children, and what a time they were having!

"Old Dame Slap must be in the larder still," said Moon-Face. "Yes, listen — I believe I can still hear her hammering away!"

Sure enough, over all the noise made by the school-children, there came the sound of hammering!

"Hadn't we better go and set her free?" said Fanny, rather alarmed. "She might stay there for ages and starve to death!"

"Don't be silly! How can she starve when she is surrounded by food of all kinds?" said

Moon-Face. "It will be the children who will go hungry! I guess when they are hungry enough they will open the larder door and let Dame Slap out all right! Goodness, what a temper she will be in."

They all hurried through the Land at top speed, half afraid that Dame Slap might be let out before they were safe, and come after them. Still, they had Mrs. Saucepan with them, and if anyone had to stand up to Dame Slap, she certainly would.

They came at last to the ladder sticking up into the Land from the cloud below. "You go first, Moon-Face, and help Mrs. Saucepan down," said Jo. So down went Moon-Face, and politely and carefully helped the old lady down the little yellow ladder, through the cloud and on to the topmost branch of the tree.

Everyone followed, breathing sighs of relief to be safely away from Dame Slap once more. Nobody ever wanted to visit *her* Land again!

"We really must say good-bye now," said Jo to the Tree-Folk. "Shall we just take Mrs. Saucepan down to Dame Washalot for you, Saucepan?"

"I'll come too," said Saucepan, hearing what was said. So down they went, and when Dame Washalot saw old Mrs. Saucepan, she was most excited. She threw her soapy arms round the old lady's neck and hugged her.

"I hope you've come to stay!" she said. "I've always wanted you to live in the Faraway Tree."

"Good-bye, Mrs. Saucepan," said Bessie. "I shall come and buy your cakes the very first day you sell them. I do hope you've had a happy birthday."

"The nicest one I've ever had!" said the old lady, beaming. "Good-bye, my dears, and hurry home!"

16.

In the Land of Secrets

Connie could not forget the exciting Faraway Tree, and the different Lands that came at the top. She asked the others about all the different Lands they had been to, and begged and begged them to take her to the next one.

"We'll see what Moon-Face says," said Jo at last. "We don't go to every Land, Connie. You wouldn't like to go to the Land of Whizz-About, for instance, would you? Moon-Face once went there, and he said he couldn't bear it—everything went at such a pace, and he was out of breath the whole time."

"Well, I think it sounds rather exciting," said Connie, who was intensely curious about everything to do with the different Lands. "Oh, Jo, do let's find out what Land is there next. I really must go."

"All right!" said Jo. "We'll ask Mother if we can have the day off to-morrow, and we'll go up the Tree if you like. But mind—if there is a horrid Land, we're not going. We've had too many narrow escapes now, to risk getting caught somewhere nasty."

Mother said they might go up the Tree the next day. "I'll give you sandwiches, if you like, and you can have dinner in the Wood or up the Tree, whichever you like," she told them.

"Oh, up the Tree!" cried Connie. So, when the next day came, she wore old clothes without even being told! She was learning to be sensible at last.

They set off soon after breakfast. They hadn't let Silky or Moon-Face know they were coming, but they felt sure they would be in the Tree.

They jumped over the ditch and made their way through the whispering wood till they came to the Faraway Tree. Jo whistled for the red squirrel to tell him to go up and ask Moon-Face to send cushions down. But the red squirrel didn't come.

"Bother!" said Bessie. "Now we'll have to climb up, and it's so hot!"

So up they climbed. The Angry Pixie was sitting at his window, which was wide open. He waved to them, and Connie was glad to see he had no ink or water to throw at her.

"Going up to the Land of Secrets?" he shouted to them.

"Oh—is the Land of Secrets there?" cried Jo. "It sounds exciting. What's it like?"

"Oh—just Secrets!" said the Angry Pixie. "You can usually find out anything you badly want to know. I believe Watzisname wanted to try and find out exactly what his real name is, so maybe he'll visit it too."

"I'd like to know some secrets too," said Connie.

"What Secrets do you want to know?" asked Jo.

"Oh—I'd like to know how much money the old man who lives next door to us at home has got," said Connie. "And I'd like to know what Mrs. Toms at home has done to make people not speak to her—and . . ."

"What an awful girl you are!" said Bessie. "Those are *other* people's Secrets, not yours. Fancy wanting to find out other people's Secrets!"

"Yes, it's horrid of you, Connie," said Fanny. "Jo, don't let Connie go into the Land of Secrets if that's the kind of thing she wants to find out. She's gone all curious and prying again, like she used to be."

Connie was angry. She went red and glared at the others. "Well, don't *you* want to know Secrets too?" she said. "You said you did!"

"Yes, but not other people's," said Jo at once. "I'd like to know where to find the very first violets for instance, so that I could surprise Mother on her birthday with a great big bunch. They are her favourite flowers."

"And I'd like to know the Secret of Curly Hair, so that I could use it on all my dolls," said Bessie.

"And I'd like to know the Secret of growing lettuces with big hearts," said Fanny. "Mine never grow nice ones."

"What awfully silly secrets!" said Connie.

"Better to want to know a silly secret than a horrid one, or one that doesn't belong to you," said Jo. "All you want to do is to poke your nose into other people's affairs, Connie, and that's a horrid thing to do."

Connie climbed the Tree, not speaking a word to the others. She was very angry with them. She was so angry that she didn't look out for Dame Washalot's water coming down the Tree, and it suddenly swished all round her and soaked her dress.

That made her crosser still, especially when the others laughed at her. "All right!" said Connie, in a nasty voice. "I'll find out *your* Secrets too— where you've put your new book so that I can't borrow it, Jo—and where you've put your big rubber, Bessie—and I'll find out which of your dolls you like the best, Fanny, and smack her hard!"

"You really are a nasty child," said Jo. "You won't go up into the Land of Secrets, so don't worry yourself about all these things!"

They climbed up to Silky's house, but it was shut. They went up to Moon-Face's, but dear me! his door was shut too. The Old Saucepan Man was not about and neither was Watzisname. Nobody seemed about at all.

"Perhaps Saucepan's mother would know," said Bessie. So they climbed down to Dame Washalot, and found old Mrs. Saucepan there.

"Saucepan and Watzisname have both gone up into the Land of Secrets," she told them, "but I don't know about Silky and Moon-Face—I expect they have gone with them, though Saucepan didn't tell me they were going. Have a bun?"

Old Mrs. Saucepan was already busy making all kinds of delicious buns and biscuits, ready to open her shop on Dame Washalot's broad branch. Two goblins were busy making a stall for her. She meant to open her little shop the next day.

The children took their buns with thanks. They were really delicious.

They climbed up the Tree again to Moon-Face's house. Jo turned the handle. The door opened, but the curved room inside was empty.

"What a nuisance!" said Jo. "Now what shall we do?"

"We might as well go up into the Land of Secrets, and find the others, and have our picnic with them," said Fanny.

"Yes," said Connie, who was dying to go up into this new Land.

"Well, but we didn't want Connie to go," said Jo. "She'll only go prying into other people's Secrets, and we can't have that."

"I won't try and find out your Secrets," said Connie. "I promise I won't."

"I don't know if I trust you," said Jo. "But still, we can't go without you. So, if you come, Connie, just be careful — and do remember that you may get into trouble if you act stupidly."

"I wonder if old Watzisname has found out what his real name is," said Bessie, beginning to climb up the topmost branch. "I'd love to know it. It would be nice to call him something else. Watzisname is a silly name."

They all went up the topmost branch, and up

the yellow ladder through the hole in the vast cloud, and then into the Land of Secrets.

It was a curious Land, quiet, perfectly still, and a sort of twilight hung over it. There was no sun to be seen at all.

"It feels secret and solemn!" said Jo, with a little shiver. "I'm not sure if I like it."

"Come on!" said Bessie. "Let's go and find the others and see how we get to know Secrets."

They came to a hill, in which were several coloured doors, set with sparkling stones that glittered in the curious twilight.

"They must be the doors of caves," said Jo. "Look!—there are names on the doors."

The children read them. They were queer names. "Witch Know-a-Lot." "The Enchanter Wise-Man." "Dame Tell-You-All." "Mrs. Hidden." "The Wizard Tall-Hat."

"They all sound awfully clever and wise and learned," said Jo. "Hallo! Here's somebody coming."

A tall elf was coming along, carrying a pair of wings. She stopped and spoke to the children.

"Do you know where 'Dame Tell-You-All' lives, please? I want to know how to fasten on these wings and fly with them."

"She lives in that cave," said Bessie, pointing to where a door had "Dame Tell-You-All" painted on it in big curly letters.

"Thank you," said the elf, and rapped sharply at the door. It opened and she went inside. It shut. In about half a minute it opened again, and out came the elf, this time with the wings on her back. She rose into the air and flew off, waving to the children.

"The Dame's awfully clever!" she cried. "I can fly now. Look!"

"This is an exciting place," said Bessie. "Goodness, the things we could learn! I wish *I* had a pair of wings. I've a good mind to go and ask Dame Tell-You-All how to get some, and then how to fly with them."

"Look!—isn't that old Watzisname coming along?" said Jo, suddenly. They looked in the dim distance, and saw that it was indeed Watzisname, looking rather proud. Saucepan was with him, his pans clashing as usual.

"Hi, Watzisname!" called Jo, loudly.

Watzisname came up. "My name is not Watzisname," he said a little haughtily. "I've at last found out what it is. It is a perfectly marvellous name."

"What is it?" asked Bessie.

"It is Kollamoolitoomarellipawkyrollo," said Watzisname, very proudly indeed. "In future please call me by my real name."

"Oh dear—I shall never remember that," said Fanny, and she tried to say it. But she didn't get any further than "Kollamooli." Nor did the others.

"No wonder everyone called him 'Watzisname'," said Bessie to Fanny. "Watzisname, where are Silky and Moon-Face?"

"My name is not Watzisname," said Watzisname, patiently. "I have told you what it is. Please address me correctly in future."

"He's gone all high-and-mighty," said Jo. "Saucepan, WHERE ARE SILKY AND MOON-FACE?"

"Don't know," said Saucepan, "and don't shout at me like that. I haven't seen Silky or Moon-Face to-day."

"Let's have our picnic here, and then go and see if Silky and Moon-Face have come home," said Jo. "I don't think somehow we'll go about finding out Secrets. This Land is a bit too mysterious for me!"

But Connie made up her mind *she* would find a few Secrets! She would have a bit of fun on her own.

17.

Connie in Trouble

They all sat down on a flowery bank. It was still twilight, which seemed very queer, as Jo's watch said the time was half-past twelve in the middle of the day. As they ate, they watched the different visitors coming and going to the cave on the hillside.

There was an old woman who wanted to ask Witch Know-a-Lot the secret of youth, so that she might become young again, and there was a tiny goblin who had once done a wicked thing, and couldn't forget it. He wanted to know the Secret of forgetting, and that is one of the most difficult secrets in the world if you have done something really bad.

The children talked to everyone who passed. It was queer, the different Secrets that people wanted to know. One cross-looking brownie wanted to know the secret of laughter.

"I've never laughed in my life," he told Jo. "And I'd like to. But nothing ever seems funny to me. Perhaps the Enchanter Wise-Man can tell me. He's very, very clever."

The Enchanter plainly knew the secret of laughter because, when the cross-looking brownie came out of the cave he was smiling. He roared with laughter as he passed the picnicking party.

"Such a joke!" he said to them. "Such a joke!"

"What was the Secret?" asked Connie.

"Ah, that's nothing to do with you!" said the brownie. "That's *my* Secret, not yours!"

The tiny goblin who had once done a wicked thing came up to the children. "Did you find out the Secret of Forgetting?" asked Bessie.

The goblin nodded.

"I'll tell it to you, because then if you do a wrong thing, maybe you can get right with yourself afterwards," he said. "It's so dreadful if you can't. Well, the Wizard Tall-Hat told me that if I can do one hundred really kind deeds to make up for the one very bad one I did, maybe I'll be able to forget a little, and think better of myself. So I'm off to do my first kind deed."

"Goodness! It'll take him a long time to make up for his one wicked deed," said Jo. "Poor little goblin! It must be awful to do something wicked and not be able to forget it. No wonder he looked unhappy."

A very grand fairy came flying down to the hillside. She looked rich and mighty and very beautiful. Connie wondered what Secret she had come to find out. It must be a very fine Secret indeed. The fairy did not tell the children what she wanted to know. She smiled at them and went to knock on Mrs. Hidden's door.

"Ah! – did you see that fairy?" said Watzisname. "It would be interesting to know what secret *she* is after! She has beauty and wealth and power – whatever Secret can she want now?"

"What do you think she wants to know, Watzisname?" asked Connie.

"Call me by my proper name and I might tell you," said Watzisname, haughtily. But Connie couldn't remember it. Nor could the others.

"Well, it isn't going to be much use finding out my real name, if nobody is going to bother to remember it," said Watzisname, in a huff. "Saucepan, do *you* remember my name?"

"Shame? Yes, it is a shame," said Saucepan.

In the middle of all the explanations to Saucepan as to what Watzisname had really said, Connie slipped away unseen. She was longing to know what Secret the beautiful fairy wanted to find out. It must be a very powerful Secret. If only she could hear it! Perhaps if she listened outside Mrs. Hidden's door, she might catch a few words.

She went off very quietly without being seen,

and climbed a little way up the hillside to where she had noticed Mrs. Hidden's door.

There it was—a pale green one, striped with red lines and a curious pattern. It was open!

Connie crept up to it. She could hear voices inside.

She stood in the doorway and peeped inside. There was a winding passage leading into the hill from the doorway. She crept down it. She turned a corner and found herself looking into a very curious room. It was small, and yet it looked very, very big because when Connie looked at the corners they faded away and weren't there.

It was the same with the ceiling, which Connie felt sure was very low. But when she looked up at it it wasn't there either! There didn't seem to be any end or beginning to the room at all, and yet Connie knew that it was small.

It gave her an uncomfortable feeling, as if she was in a dream. She tried to see Mrs. Hidden. She could see the beautiful fairy quite well, and she could hear Mrs. Hidden, whoever she was, speaking in a low, deep voice.

But she couldn't see her!

"Oh well—I suppose she's called Mrs. Hidden because she is hidden from our sight," thought Connie. "I will just hear what she says to the fairy, and then slip away."

Connie heard the Secret that the beautiful fairy wanted to know, and she heard Mrs. Hidden give her the answer. Connie shivered with delight. It was a very wonderful and powerful Secret.

Connie meant to use it herself! She began to creep out of the cave.

But her foot caught against a loose stone in the passage and it made a noise. At once Mrs. Hidden called out in a sharp voice: "Who's there? Who's prying and peeping? Who's listening? I'll put a spell on you, I will! If you have heard any Secrets, you will not be able to speak again!"

Connie fled, afraid of having a Spell put on her. She came rushing down the hillside, her face very frightened. The others heard her and frowned.

"Connie! Surely you haven't been after Secrets when we said you were not to try and find out anything?" began Jo.

Connie opened her mouth to answer—but not a word came out! Not one single word!

"She can't speak," said Watzisname. "She's been listening at doors and hearing things not meant for her ears. I guess old Mrs. Hidden has put a spell on her. Serve her right."

Connie opened her mouth and tried to speak again, pointing back to the cave she had come from. Saucepan got up in a hurry.

"I can see what she means to say," he said to the others. "She's been caught prying and peeping, and she's afraid Mrs. Hidden will come after her. She probably will as soon as she has finished with that beautiful fairy who went into her cave. We'd better go. Mrs. Hidden is not a nice person to deal with when she is angry."

They all ran to the hole, and got down it as quickly as possible. Connie was so anxious to get away from Mrs. Hidden that she almost fell off the topmost branch. Jo caught her dress just in time.

"Look out!" he said. "You nearly went headlong down the Tree. Let me go first."

Connie couldn't answer. Mrs. Hidden's spell was plainly very strong. She simply couldn't say a word. It was very queer, and very horrid.

"I say—do you suppose Silky and Moon-Face are still up there in the Land of Secrets?" asked Bessie. But they weren't, for as they came down the branch to Moon-Face's house, they heard voices, and saw Silky and Moon-Face undoing parcels of shopping.

"Oh—so you went shopping, did you?" said Jo. "We wondered where you were."

"Yes, we took the little red squirrel shopping and bought him a new jersey," said Moon-Face. "He's terribly pleased. I say—did you go up into the Land of Secrets? Did you find out anything?"

"Yes, we found out Watzisname's real name," said Jo.

"Oh, *good!*" said Silky. "I've always wanted to know it. What is it, Jo?"

Jo wrinkled up his forehead. "I can't remember," he said.

"What's the good of a name nobody remembers?" said Watzisname, gloomily. "It's just stupid."

"You tell me it, and I'll promise to remember," said Silky. "I'll write it down and learn it by heart, Watzisname, really I will."

Watzisname said nothing. Silky gave him a little poke. "Go on, Watzisname. Tell me your name — slowly, now, so that I can say it after you."

Watzisname shook his head, and suddenly looked miserable. "I — I can't tell you my name," he said at last. "I've forgotten it myself! It was such a fine name too. You'll have to call me Watzisname just the same as before. I expect that's why people *did* begin to call me Watzisname, because nobody could ever remember my real name."

"Well, it's a pity to think that the only Secret we found out has been forgotten already!" said Jo. "Though I suppose Connie found out a Secret she wasn't supposed to know and got punished for it. Moon-Face, Connie can't speak. Isn't it awful?"

"Good thing," said Saucepan, hearing unexpectedly. "Never says anything really sensible."

Connie glared at him and opened her mouth to say something sharp. But no words came.

Silky looked at her in sympathy.

"Poor Connie! Whatever can we do about it? We'll have to wait till the Land of Enchantments comes, and then go up and find someone who can take the spell away. *I* don't know how to make you better."

"Why bother?" said Saucepan, quite enjoying Connie's anger at being unable to answer him back. "Why bother? She'll be much nicer if she can't say a word. We shan't know she's there!"

"Never mind, Connie," said Bessie, seeing that

Connie looked really upset. "As soon as the Land of Enchantments comes, we'll take you there and have you put right!"

18.

Off to Find Connie's Lost Voice

Mother was surprised to find that Connie couldn't speak, and very much alarmed.

"We'd better take her to the doctor," she said.

"Oh no, Mother, that's no use," said Jo. "It's a spell that Mrs. Hidden put on Connie for hearing something she shouldn't have listened to. Only another spell can put her right."

"When the Land of Enchantments comes we will take Connie there, and see if we can find someone who will give her her voice back again," said Bessie.

"She'll have to be patient till then," said Fanny. But Connie wasn't patient. She kept opening her mouth to try and speak, but she couldn't say a word.

"Connie shouldn't be so curious," said Jo. "It's her own fault she's like this. Perhaps it will teach her a lesson."

Three days went by, and no news came from the Tree-Folk. Then old Mrs. Saucepan arrived, with a basket full of lovely new-made cakes for the children's mother.

"I have heard so much about you," she said to

their mother, smiling all over her apple-cheeked face. "I felt I must come and call on you, Madam, and bring you a few of my cakes. I have started a shop up the Tree, near Dame Washalot, and should be so pleased to serve you, if I could."

"Stop and have tea with us, and we'll try your cakes," said Mother at once. She liked the little old lady very much. So Mrs. Saucepan stopped and had tea. She shook her head when she saw that Connie still could not speak.

"A pity," she said. "A great pity. It just doesn't do to poke your nose into other people's affairs. I hope the poor child will be put right soon. The Land of Enchantments will be at the top of the Tree to-morrow."

Everyone sat up. "What, so soon?" said Jo. "That's a bit of luck for Connie."

"It is," said old Mrs. Saucepan. "Still, there are plenty of lands where she might get her voice put right. You'll have to be just a bit careful in the Land of Enchantments, though. It's so easy to get enchanted there, without knowing it."

"Whatever do you mean?" said Mother, in alarm. "I don't think I want the children to go there, if there is any danger."

"I'll send Saucepan with them," said the old lady. "I'll give him a powerful spell, which will get anyone out of an enchantment if they get into it by mistake. You needn't worry."

"Oh, that's all right then," said Jo. "I didn't want to get enchanted, and have to stay up there for the rest of my life!"

"You must remember one or two things," said Mrs. Saucepan. "*Don't* step into a ring drawn on the ground in chalk. Don't stroke any black cats with green eyes. And don't be rude to anyone at all."

"We'll remember," said Jo. "Thank you very much. Will you tell Saucepan we'll be up the Tree to-morrow, please?"

Old Mrs. Saucepan left after tea, having made firm friends with Mother, who promised to send the children once a week to buy new cakes.

"We'll go to the Land of Enchantments to-morrow," said Jo. "Cheer up, Connie—you'll soon get your voice back!"

The next day was very rainy, and Mother didn't want the children to go up the Tree. But Connie's eyes filled with tears, and Mother saw how badly she longed to go.

"Well, put on your macs," she said, "and take umbrellas. Then you'll be all right. It may not be raining in the Land of Enchantments. And do remember what Mrs. Saucepan said, Jo, and be very careful."

"We'll be careful," said Jo, putting on his old mackintosh. "No treading in chalk rings—no stroking of black cats with green eyes—and no rudeness from anyone!"

Off they went. The Tree was very slippery to climb, because it was so wet. Somebody had run a thick rope all the way down it, and the children were glad to hold on to it as they went up the Tree. The Angry Pixie was in a temper that morning

129

because the rain had come in at his window and made puddles on the floor. He was scooping up the water and throwing it out of the window

"Look out!" said Jo. "Go round the other side of the Tree. The Angry Pixie's in a rage."

Silky was not at home. Dame Washalot for once in a way was doing no washing, because it really was too wet to dry it. So she was helping Mrs. Saucepan to bake cakes on her little stove inside the Tree. The children got a hot bun each.

Saucepan and Silky were at Moon-Face's house waiting for the children to come. "Where's Watzisname?" said Jo.

"Gone to sleep," said Moon-Face. "Didn't you see him on the way up? Oh no—he would be indoors on a day like this, of course. He sat up half the night trying to remember his real name and write it down so that he wouldn't forget it again. So he was very sleepy this morning. And he didn't remember his name of course."

"Is the Land of Enchantments up there?" said Jo, nodding his head towards the top of the tree.

"It must be," said Silky. "I've met two witches and two enchanters coming down the Tree to-day. They don't live here, so they must have come down from the Land of Enchantments."

"They come down to get the scarlet-spotted toadstools that grow in the Enchanted Wood," said Saucepan. "They are very magic, you know, and can be used in hundreds of spells."

"There goes an old wizard or enchanter now," said Silky, as someone in a tall pointed hat went

down past Moon-Face's door. "Shall we go now? I'm sure Connie will be glad to get her voice back."

Connie nodded. But she suddenly remembered what Mrs. Saucepan had said—that she would give Saucepan a very powerful spell, so that if any of them got caught in an enchantment, Saucepan could set them free by using his spell.

But she couldn't say all this, of course. So she pulled out the note-book she had been using for messages and scribbled something on one of the pages. She showed it to Jo.

"What about the spell that Saucepan was going to take with him?"

"Oh my goodness, yes," said Jo, and he turned to Saucepan. "Did your mother give you a powerful spell to take with you, Saucepan, in case we get caught in an enchantment?"

"My gracious!" said Saucepan, beginning to look all round him in a hurry. "Where did I put it? Silky, have you seen it? What did I do with it?"

"You really are a silly, Saucepan," said Silky, looking everywhere. "You know it's a spell that can move about. It's no use putting it down for a minute, because it will only move off somewhere."

The spell was found at last. It was a funny round red spell, with little things that stuck out all round it rather like spiders' legs. It could move about with these, and had walked off Moon-Face's mantelpiece, and settled itself down at the edge of the Slippery-Slip.

"Look at that!" said Saucepan, snatching it up quickly. "Another inch and it would have been down the Slippery-Slip and gone for ever. Wherever shall I put it for safety?"

"In a kettle, and put the lid on," said Jo. So into a kettle went the spell, and the lid was put on as tightly as could be.

"It's safe now," said Saucepan. "Come on — up we go — and be careful, everyone!"

They all left their umbrellas and macs behind, and up into the Land of Enchantments they went. It wasn't a twilight Land like the Land of Secrets; it was a land of strange colours and lights and shadows. Everything shone and shimmered and moved. Nothing stayed the same for more than a moment. It was beautiful and strange.

There were curious little shops everywhere where witches, enchanters and goblins cried their wares. There was a shining palace that looked as if it was made of glass, and towered up into the sky. The Enchanter Mighty-One lived there. He was head of the whole Land.

There were magic cloaks for sale, that could make anyone invisible at once. How Jo longed to buy one! There were silver wands full of magic. There were enchantments for everything!

"Spell to turn your enemy into a spider," cried a black goblin. "Spell to enchant a bird to your hand! Spell to understand the whispering of the trees!"

The spells and enchantments were very expensive. Nobody could possibly buy them, for no one in the little company had more than a few pence in their pockets. Even the cheapest spell cost a sack of gold!

"Oh, look at all those pixies dancing in a ring and singing as they dance!" said Bessie, turning her head as she saw a party of bright-winged pixies capering in a ring together.

She went over to watch them, and they smiled at her and held out their hands. "Come and dance too, little girl!" they cried.

Bessie didn't see that they were all dancing inside a ring drawn on the ground in white chalk! In a trice she was in the ring too, linking hands with the pixies and dancing round and round!

The others watched, smiling. Then Jo gave a

cry of horror, and pointed to the ground.

"Bessie's gone into a ring! Bessie, come out, quick!"

Bessie looked alarmed. She dropped the hands of the pixies, and came to the edge of the ring. But alas, poor Bessie couldn't jump over it! She was a prisoner in the magic ring.

"Saucepan, get out the spell at once, the one your mother gave you!" cried Jo. "Quick, quick! Before anything happens to Bessie. She may be getting enchanted."

Saucepan took the lid off the kettle into which he had put the Spell. He put in his hand and groped round. He groped and he groped, an alarmed look coming on his face.

"Saucepan, be *quick*!" said Jo.

"The Spell has gone!" said Saucepan dolefully. "Look in the kettle, Jo—the Spell isn't there. I can't get Bessie out of the magic ring!"

19.

The Land of Enchantments

Everyone stared at Saucepan in horror.

"Saucepan! The Spell can't be gone! Why, you put the lid on as tightly as can be," said Silky. "Let *me* look!"

Everyone looked, but it was quite plain to see that the kettle was empty. There was no spell there.

"Well, maybe you didn't put it into that kettle, but into another one," said Jo. "You've got so many hanging round you. Look in another kettle, Saucepan."

So Saucepan looked into every one of his kettles, big and small, and even into his saucepans too — but that Spell was not to be found.

"It's really most peculiar," said Moon-Face, puzzled. "I don't see how it could possibly have got out! Oh dear — why didn't one of us keep the Spell instead of Saucepan? We might have known he would lose it!"

"We're in real danger in this strange Land, without a Spell to protect us," said Silky. "But we can't run off home because we mustn't leave Bessie in a magic ring, and we have to try and get Connie put right. Oh dear!"

"We'll have to find someone who will get Bessie out of the ring," said Jo, anxiously. "Let's go round the Land of Enchantments and see if anyone will help us."

So they started off, leaving poor Bessie looking sadly after them. But the pixies took her hands and made her dance once again.

The children came to a small shop at the back of which sat a goblin with green ears and eyes. In front of him were piled boxes and bottles of all sorts, some with such strange spells in them that they shimmered as if they were alive.

"Could you help us?" said Jo, politely. "Our sister has got into a magic ring by mistake, and we want to get her out."

The goblin grinned. "Oh no, I'm not helping you to get her out!" he said. "Magic rings are one of our little traps to keep people here."

"You're a very nasty person then," said Moon-Face, who was upset because he was very fond of Bessie.

The goblin glared at him and moved his big green ears backwards and forwards like a dog.

"How dare you call me names?" he said. "I'll turn you into a gramophone that can do nothing but call rude names, if you're not careful."

"Indeed you won't," said Moon-Face, getting angry. "What a silly little goblin like you daring to put a spell on me, the great Moon-Face! You think too much of yourself, little green-ears. Go and bury yourself in the garden!"

"Moon-Face!" said Fanny, suddenly. "Don't be rude. Remember what Mrs. Saucepan said."

But it was too late. Moon-Face had been rude and now he was in the goblin's power. When the green-eared little creature beckoned slyly to him, poor Moon-Face found that his legs took him to the goblin, no matter how he tried not to go.

"You'll be my servant now, great Moon-Face!" said the goblin. "Now, just begin a little work, please. Sort out those boxes into their right sizes for me. And remember, no more rudeness."

Fanny burst into tears. She couldn't bear to see Moon-Face doing what the nasty little goblin said. "Oh, Saucepan, why did you lose that spell?" she wailed. "Why did you?"

"Here's a powerful-looking enchanter," said

Jo, as a tall man in a great flowing cloak swept by. "Maybe he could help us."

He stopped the Enchanter and spoke to him. A fine black cat came out from the tall man's shimmering cloak, and strolled over to Silky, blinking his great green eyes at her.

"Can you help us, please?" asked Jo, politely. "Some of our friends are in difficulties here."

He was just going on to explain, when he suddenly stopped and made a dart at Silky who was stroking the black cat and saying sweet things to it! She was very fond of cats, and stroked every one she saw. But she mustn't—she mustn't do that in the Land of Enchantments!

It was too late. She had done it. Now she had to follow the Enchanter, who smiled lazily round at the little company. "A nice little elf!" he said to them. "I shall like having her around with the black cat. She will be company for him. She can cook the mice he catches. He won't eat them raw."

To the great dismay of the others, the Enchanter swept off, his cloak flowing out and covering poor Silky and the cat.

"Oh, now Silky's gone!" sobbed Fanny. "First it was Bessie, then Moon-Face, and now Silky. Whatever are we to do?"

"Look!" said Saucepan, suddenly, and he pointed to a little shop nearby. On it was painted a sentence in yellow paint:

"Come here to get things you have lost!"

"What about trying to get Connie's voice there," said Saucepan. "Not that *I* want her to have her

voice back; I think she's much nicer without it—
but we might be able to get it back if we go to
that shop."

They went over to it, Fanny still wiping her eyes.
The shop was kept by the same beautiful fairy who
had flown to Mrs. Hidden's cave, and whose secret
Connie had overheard! Connie was afraid of going
to her, but Saucepan pulled her over to the shop.

The beautiful fairy knew Saucepan, and was
delighted to see him. When he told her about
Connie, she looked grave. "Yes, I know all about
it," she said. "It was *my* Secret she heard, and a
very wonderful Secret it was. Has she written it
down to tell any of you?"

Connie shook her head. She took out her little
notebook and wrote in it. She tore out the page
and gave it to the fairy.

"I am terribly sorry for what I did," the fairy
read. "Please forgive me. I haven't told the
Secret, and I never will. If you will give me back
my lost voice, I promise never to peep and pry
again, or to try and overhear things not meant for
me."

"I will forgive you," said the fairy, gravely.
"But, Connie, if ever you do tell the Secret, I am
afraid your voice will be lost again and will never
come back. Look! I will give it back to you now—
but remember to be careful in future."

She handed Connie a little bottle of blue and
yellow liquid, and a small red glass. "Drink what
is in the bottle," she said. "Your voice is there. It's
a good thing I didn't sell it to anyone."

138

Connie poured out the curious liquid and drank it. It tasted bitter, and she made a face.

"Oh, how horrid!" she cried, and then clapped her hands in joy. "I can speak! My voice is back! Oh, I can talk!"

"It's a pity!" said Saucepan. "I like you better when you don't talk. Still, I needn't listen."

Connie was so excited at having her voice back again that she talked and talked without stopping. The others were very silent. Both Jo and Saucepan were worried, and Fanny was still crying.

"Be quiet, Connie!" said Jo at last. "Saucepan, WHAT SHALL WE DO?"

"Go back and ask my mother for another spell," said Saucepan. "That's the best I can think of."

So they all went back to the hole in the clouds. But they couldn't get down it because there were so many people coming up!

"The Land of Enchantments must be moving away again soon," said Saucepan, in dismay. "Look! Everyone is hurrying back to it, with their toadstools and things!"

"We can't risk going down to your mother then," said Jo, more worried than ever. "If the Land moves on it will take Moon-Face, Bessie and Silky with it, and we shall never see them again."

They sat down at the edge of the hole, and looked worried and upset. What in the world were they to do?

Then Fanny gave such a loud cry that everyone jumped hard. "What's that? What's that sticking out of the spout of that kettle, Saucepan? Something red, waving about—look!"

Everyone looked—and Saucepan gave a yell. "It's the Spell! It must have crawled up the spout, and that's why we didn't see it when we looked in the kettle! It couldn't get out because the spout is too small. Those are its leg-things waving about, trying to get out of the spout!"

"Quick! Get it out, Saucepan," said Jo.

"Bad spell, naughty Spell," said Saucepan, severely, and poked his finger in the spout, pushing the spell right back. It fell with a little thud into the inside of the kettle. In a trice Saucepan took off the lid, put in his hand and grabbed the spell. He jumped to his feet.

"Come on! Maybe we've just got time to rescue the others, Bessie first!"

They rushed to the magic ring, and Saucepan stepped into it with the spell held firmly in his hand. At once the chalk ring faded away, the pixies ran off squealing, and Bessie was free. How she hugged Saucepan!

"No time to waste, no time to waste," said Saucepan, and ran off to find Silky. He saw the Enchanter in his floating cloak, talking to a witch, and rushed up to him.

"Silky, Silky, where are you? I've a spell to set you free!" cried Saucepan.

The Enchanter looked down and saw the wriggling red spell in Saucepan's hand. He shook out his cloak and Silky at once appeared. Saucepan clutched her by the hand.

"Come on! You're free. You don't need to follow him any more. He's afraid of this spell."

The Enchanter certainly was. He ran off with his black cat without a word.

"Now for Moon-Face," said Saucepan. "Gracious, can I hear the humming noise that means this Land will soon be on the move?"

He could, and so could the others. With beating hearts they rushed to the green-eared goblin's shop. There was no time to waste. Saucepan threw the red spell at the goblin, and it went down his neck.

"You're free, Moon-Face. Come quickly!" cried Saucepan. "The Land is on the move!"

Moon-Face rushed after the others, leaving the goblin to try and grope the wriggling spell out of his neck. Everyone rushed to the hole that led down through the cloud. The Land was shaking a little already, as if it was just going to move.

Bessie and Fanny were pushed down quickly. Then Silky and Connie followed, almost falling down in their hurry. Then came Moon-Face and Jo, and last of all Saucepan, who nearly got stuck in the hole with his saucepans and kettles. He got free and fell down with a bump.

"The Land's just off!" he cried, as a creaking sound came down the ladder. "We only just escaped in time! Goodness, look how I've dented my kettles!"

20

What is Wrong with the Faraway Tree?

Connie was very talkative for a few days after they had been to the Land of Enchantments. It seemed as if she had to keep on making sure she had her voice once more.

"Well, I half wish you'd lose it again," said Jo, when Connie had talked for about ten minutes. "Do let someone else get a word in, Connie!"

"We'll have to take her to the Land of Silence!" said Bessie. "Then she'll be quiet for a bit."

"What's the Land of Silence?" said Connie, who really loved to hear of all the different Lands that came to the top of the Tree.

"I don't know. I only just thought of it," said Bessie, laughing. "It may not be a Land at the top of the Tree for all I know!"

"I wonder what Land is there now," said Connie. "When are we going to see, Jo?"

"There's no hurry," said Jo. "You know Silky and Moon-Face have gone away to stay for a bit, so they aren't in the Tree. We'll wait till they come back."

"They'll be back on Thursday," said Fanny. "We'll go and see them then. We'll stop and buy some of Mrs. Saucepan's cakes, and take them up to Moon-Face's for tea. Mother, can we go on Thursday?"

"Yes," said Mother. "I'll make some ginger biscuits for you to take, too."

Connie could hardly wait till Thursday came. Jo laughed at her. "Well, considering that you jeered at the Enchanted Wood, and didn't believe in the Faraway Tree or any of the folk in it, to say nothing of the Lands at the top, it's funny that you're keener than any of us to visit there now!" said Jo.

Thursday came. After their dinner the children packed up Mother's lovely ginger biscuits, and set off to the Enchanted Wood. They jumped over the ditch and landed in the quiet wood. The trees were whispering together loudly.

"They seem to be louder than usual," said Jo. "They seem sort of excited to-day. I wonder if anything has happened!"

"Wisha, wisha, wisha," whispered the trees together, and waved their branches up and down. "Wisha-wisha, wisha-wisha!"

The children walked to the Faraway Tree. There it was, enormous, its great trunk towering upwards, and its wide-spreading branches waving in the wind.

Jo gave a little cry of surprise.

"What's happening to the Tree? Look, some of its leaves are curling up—sort of withering. Surely it isn't going to shed its leaves yet."

"Well, it's only summer-time," said Bessie, feeling the leaves. "Don't they feel dry and dead? I wonder what has happened to make them go like this."

"Perhaps the leaves will be all right a bit higher up," said Connie. "It's growing no fruit of any sort down here, is it? That's rather unusual."

It certainly was. The Faraway Tree as a rule grew all kinds of different fruits all the way up. It might begin with lemons, go on to pears, load itself a bit higher up with peaches, and end up with acorns. You never knew what it would grow, but it certainly grew something.

Now to-day there was no fruit to be seen, only withering leaves. Jo leapt up on to the first branch. Up he went to the next and the next, but all the way up the leaves seemed to be withering and dying. It was curious and rather alarming. The Faraway Tree was magic—something very serious must be the matter if the leaves were dying.

"That's the first sign that a tree itself is dying, if the leaves wither," said Jo. The others looked upset. They loved the Faraway Tree, and all its little Tree-folk. It wasn't only a tree, it was a home for many queer little people—and the path to strange adventures far above.

The Angry Pixie was in his room. Jo rapped on the window, and the Pixie picked up a jug of water to throw. But he put it down again when he saw it was Jo.

"Hallo!" he said. "Are you on your way to Moon-Face's? He's just back."

"I say—what's the matter with the Faraway Tree?" asked Jo.

The Angry Pixie shook his head gloomily.

"Don't know," he said. "Nobody knows.

Nobody at all. It's a very serious thing. Why, the Faraway Tree should live to be a thousand years old—and it's only five hundred and fifty-three so far."

The Owl was asleep in his bed. No water came down from Dame Washalot. When the children got up as far as her branch, they saw her talking seriously to old Mrs. Saucepan, who was busy arranging stacks of new-made buns on her stall.

"Can't think what's the matter," Dame Washalot was saying. "I've been here on this branch for nearly a hundred years, and never—no, never—have I known one single leaf wither. Why, the Tree grows new ones each day, and fruit, too. Many's the time I've stripped this branch of fruit, and before I've cooked it, it has been full again of some other kind of fruit. Now there's none to be seen."

"You're right," said Mrs. Saucepan. "I've been up the Tree to the top, and down to the bottom, and not a bit of fruit is there to be seen."

"What do you think is the matter?" asked Jo, climbing up. But neither of the old women knew. Mister Watzisname was looking carefully at every curled up, withering leaf, to see if caterpillars were the cause of the trouble.

"I thought if it was caterpillars I'd send a call to all the birds in the Enchanted Wood," he said. "They would soon put things right, by eating the grubs. But it isn't caterpillars."

The children went on to Moon-Face's. He was in his curved room with Silky. But he didn't

145

beam at them as usual as he opened his door. He looked anxious and sad.

"Hallo!" he said. "How nice to see you! We've just got back—and my, what a shock we got when we saw the Tree! I believe it's dying."

"Oh *no*!" said Jo, quite shocked. "It's a magic Tree, surely?"

"Yes, but even magic Trees die if something goes wrong with them," said Moon-Face. "The thing is—no one knows what's wrong, you see. We might put it right, if we knew."

"Do you think the roots want water?" asked Bessie. Moon-Face shook his head.

"No—it's been a wet summer, and besides the Tree's roots go down very, very deep—right into some old caves deep down below. Jewels were once found there, but I don't think there are any now."

"You know," said Jo, looking serious, "my father once had a fine apple tree that suddenly went like this, all its leaves curling up. I remember quite well."

"What was the matter with it?" said Silky.

"There was something wrong with its roots," said Jo. "I don't know what. But I know my father said that when a tree's roots go wrong, the tree dies unless you can put the trouble right."

"But what could go wrong with the Faraway Tree's roots?" said Moon-Face, puzzled.

"I suppose—I suppose there couldn't be any-one down there, interfering with them, could there?" said Jo.

Moon-Face shook his head. "I shouldn't think so. No one is allowed at the roots, you know. Those old jewel-caves were closed up as soon as the Tree's roots reached to them."

"Still—it would be a good idea to find out if anything is damaging the roots," said Jo. "Could you send a rabbit down, do you think? He could tell you, couldn't he?"

"Yes. That's quite a good idea," said Moon-Face. He went to the door and whistled for the red squirrel. When the little fellow came, Moon-Face told him to fetch one of the rabbits that lived in the wood.

One soon came bounding up the Tree like the squirrel! It was odd to watch him. He was proud to be called for by Moon-Face.

"Listen, Woffles!" said Moon-Face, who knew every single rabbit in the Enchanted Wood. "Do you know your way down to the jewel-caves at the roots of the Faraway Tree?"

"Of course," said Woffles. "But the caves are closed, Mister Moon-Face. They have been for years."

"Well, we think something may be damaging the roots of the Tree," said Moon-Face. "We want you to go down as far as you can, and see if there is anything to find out. Come back and tell us as soon as you can."

"Could I—could I just go down the Slippery-Slip for once?" said the rabbit, shyly.

"Of course," said Moon-Face, and threw him a cushion. "There you are. Give it back to the red squirrel at the foot of the tree."

The rabbit shot off down the Slippery-Slip, squealing with excitement and delight.

"Isn't he sweet?" said Fanny. "I wish he was mine! I hope it won't be long before he's back. Shall we have tea, Moon-Face? We've brought some ginger biscuits from Mother, and some seed buns from Mrs. Saucepan."

They began their tea. Before they had finished the rabbit was back, looking very scared.

"Mister Moon-Face! Oh, Mister Moon-Face! Look at my bobtail! Half the hairs are gone!"

"What's happened to it?" asked Moon-Face.

"Well, I went down to the old jewel-caves, and I heard a noise of hammering and banging," said the rabbit. "I burrowed a hole to see what the noise was—and do you know, all the caves are filled with curious little people! I don't know what they are. They saw me and one caught hold of my tail and pulled nearly all the hairs out."

Everyone sat silent, staring from one to the other. People in the old jewel-caves—hammering and crashing round the roots of the Faraway Tree! No wonder it was dying. Maybe the roots were terribly damaged!

"We'll have to look into this," said Moon-Face at last. "Thank you, Woffles. Your hairs will grow again. Red Squirrel, go down the Tree and tell everyone to come up here. We must hold a Meeting. Something has Got to be Done!"

21.

Down to the Jewel-Caves

The red squirrel bounded off down the Tree to call everyone to a Meeting. "Go up to Moon-Face's," he told everyone. "There is to be an important Meeting about the Faraway Tree. Most important."

Soon everyone was on their way up the Tree to Moon-Face's house at the top. Dame Washalot arrived, panting. Behind her came old Mrs. Saucepan. Mister Watzisname came, and Saucepan too. The owl came with two friends. The woodpecker came, and two or three squirrels, with a good many baby squirrels to join in the excitement. The Angry Pixie came too, of course.

It was too much of a squash in Moon-Face's curved room, so everyone sat outside on the broad branch. Moon-Face addressed the Meeting.

"Something very serious is happening," he said. "The Faraway Tree is dying, as you can all see for yourselves. Even in the last hour or two its leaves have curled up even more. And not a single fruit or berry of any kind is to be found from top to bottom, a thing that has never happened before."

"That's true," said Dame Washalot. "I've always depended on the Tree for my pies. But now there isn't any fruit, not even a red currant."

"We have discovered that there are people in the

149

jewel-caves at the roots of the Tree," said Moon-Face, solemnly.

"Oooo-ooooh!" said everyone, in amazement.

"Woffles went down and saw them," said Moon-Face. The rabbit almost fell off the branch with pride at being mentioned by name.

"But—the jewel-caves have been closed for many years!" said Dame Washalot, in surprise.

"Yes—because the roots of the Tree went deep into them," said Moon-Face. "Anyway, I don't think there were any more jewels to be found. But plainly there are robbers who think there may be some left, and they have come after them, forced open the caves, and are damaging the roots of the Tree in their hunt for jewels. Unless we can stop them quickly, I am afraid the Faraway Tree will die."

"Oh dear—would it have to be chopped down?" said Bessie, in dismay. She couldn't bear to think of such a thing. It would be dreadful. All the children were as fond of the friendly Faraway Tree as the tree-folk themselves were.

"What are we going to do about it?" said the Angry Pixie. "I wish I could get at those robbers!"

"We'd better find out who they are first. And how many of them," said Silky. "Then we could send round the Enchanted Wood and get dozens of people to come and help us to force the robbers out of the caves. Maybe if we could stop them damaging the roots any more the Tree would recover."

"I will go down to the jewel-caves myself and speak with the robbers," said Moon-Face, his round face looking solemn. "Saucepan, will you come with me?"

"Oh yes. Of course. Without doubt," said old Saucepan at once.

"I'm coming too," said Watzisname.

"And all of us are," said the children at once, and Silky nodded as well. This looked like being a very solemn kind of adventure, but they meant to share it as usual.

"Well—I think we ought to go right away now," said Moon-Face, getting up. "No time like the present. Coming, all of you?"

"Yes," said everyone, and stood up. Connie felt thrilled. What adventures she had had since she came to stay with Jo, Bessie and Fanny!

"Where's Woffles?" said Moon-Face, looking round. "Ah, there you are! Woffles, please lead the way."

The rabbit almost burst with pride. He ran down the Tree in front of the others. Everyone followed. When they came to the ground Woffles ran to a big rabbit-hole.

"Down here," he said. So down went the children and the four Tree-Folk—down, down into the darkness. It was a good thing the rabbit-hole was so big. Rabbit burrows in the Enchanted Wood were always on the large side because the goblins, gnomes, pixies and brownies liked to use the underground tunnels when it rained.

"I've never been down a rabbit-hole before,"

said Connie. "Never! It's like a dream! I hope I shan't wake up and find it isn't real. I like this sort of thing."

So did the others. It was queer down the rabbit-hole, rather dark, and a bit musty. Woffles knew the way very well, of course. He knew every burrow in the Wood!

Here and there were queer lanterns hanging from the roof where it was a bit higher than usual, usually at sharp corners. It was a bit of a squash when anyone else came along in the opposite direction, for then everyone had to flatten themselves against the wall of the tunnel.

Quite a lot of people met them. Rabbits, of course, and brownies and goblins seemed to be hurrying about by the dozen.

"Woffles, are you sure this is the way?" said Moon-Face at last, when it seemed as if they had been wandering along dark tunnels for miles and miles. "Are you sure you are not lost?"

Woffles made rather a rude snort. "Lost! As if any rabbit is ever lost underground!" he said. "No, Mister Moon-Face, you can trust me. I never get lost here. I am taking you the very shortest way."

They went on again, groping their way along the tunnels, glad of an unexpected ray of light from a lantern now and again. And then they heard something!

"Hark!" said Moon-Face, stopping so suddenly that Jo bumped right into him. "Hark! What is that?"

Everyone stood and held their breath—and they heard queer muffled noises coming from the depths of the earth.

"Boom, boom, boom! Boom, boom, boom!"

"That's the people I told you about," said the rabbit, importantly. "We're getting near the jewel-caves."

Connie felt a bit queer. She held Watzisname's hand tightly.

"Boom, boom, boom!"

"It's the robbers all right," said Moon-Face, and his voice echoed queerly down the tunnel. "Can't you hear their pick-axes?"

"Is it safe to go on?" said Silky, doubtfully. "You don't think they'd take us prisoners or anything, do you?"

"I'll go first with Jo," said Moon-Face, "and you others can keep back in the shadows, if you like. I don't think the robbers would try to capture us. They would know that a whole army of people would come down from the Enchanted Wood after them, if they did!"

They went forward again, making as little noise as they could. Even old Saucepan hardly made a clank or a clang with his saucepans and kettles.

"Boom, boom, boom!" The sound came nearer still. "BOOM, BOOM, BOOM!"

"They are certainly working very hard," said Jo, in a whisper. "They are using pick-axes to break down the caves to see if any more precious stones are hidden there. No wonder the Tree is dying. They must be striking the roots every time."

"There's a root, look!" said Silky, and she pointed to a thick rope-like thing that jutted out into the tunnel, right across their path. It shone queerly in the light of an old lantern that swung from the roof just there.

"Yes, that's a root," said Moon-Face, climbing over it. "Be careful of it, all of you!"

So they were very careful, because they didn't want to hurt the Faraway Tree at all. It was being hurt quite enough, as it was, by the robbers.

"Now—here are the caves," said Woffles, excitedly, as they turned a corner, and came to a great door, studded with iron and brass. "You can't get through that door. It's locked."

"How did you get into the caves?" said Moon-Face. "Oh yes, I remember—you made a burrow. Where is it?"

Woffles pointed to it with his paw. But good gracious, out of it pointed something sharp and glittering! Whatever could it be?

Moon-Face stepped up to see. He came back and whispered gravely. "It's a sharp spear! The robbers plainly don't mean anyone to get into the caves again. There are three of these doors, I know—but the robbers will have locked them all —and any rabbit-hole will be guarded by them too —with spears!"

"There must be someone holding the spear," said Jo. "Let's go and talk to him! Come on, Moon-Face. We'll tell him what we think of robbers who hurt the roots of the dear old Faraway Tree!"

22.

The Rabbits Come to Help

Jo and Moon-Face walked boldly up to the rabbit-hole. It was the one Woffles had made that day, when he had gone down to inquire into things. Clearly the robbers had discovered it and were guarding it.

The shining spear moved a little, and a harsh voice cried out sharply:

"Who goes there?"

"This is Jo and Moon-Face," said Moon-Face. "We have come to tell you that you are making the Faraway Tree die, because you are damaging its roots."

"Pooh!" said the voice, rudely.

Moon-Face felt angry. "Don't you care whether or not you kill a tree?" he asked. "And the Faraway Tree, too, the finest Tree in the world!"

"We don't care a bit," said the voice. "Why should we? We don't live in the Tree. We are Trolls, who live underground. We don't care about trees."

"Trolls!" said Moon-Face. "Of course, I might have guessed it. You live under the ground and work the soil there to find gold and precious stones, don't you?"

"How clever you are!" said the mocking voice. "Now go away, please. You can't get into the caves, nor can you stop us doing what we want to. There are plenty of precious stones here still, and until we have found them all, we shall hold these caves against any enemy."

"You can have all the jewels you like if only you won't hurt the roots of the Tree," said Moon-Face, desperately.

"We can't help it," said the voice. "The roots grow through the walls, and are always getting into our way. We chop them off!"

"Gracious! No wonder the poor Tree is dying," said Jo. "Moon-Face, whatever are we to do?"

Moon-Face went a little nearer the rabbit-hole. Would it be possible to bring a whole army of Wood-Folk and force a way down the hole—or even get the rabbits to make more holes? No—it certainly wasn't possible to get down *this* hole, at any rate. Another spear had now appeared, and they were horribly sharp and pointed.

"How did you get into the caves?" shouted Moon-Face, moving back a little. "The doors were always kept locked, and the Brownie Long-Beard had the key."

"Oh, we stole it from him and got in easily!" said the voice, with a laugh. "Then we locked the doors on this side, so that no one else could get in. We've been here a week now, and nobody knew till that interfering rabbit came along. Wait till we get him! We'll cook him in our stew-pot."

Woffles fled to the back of the listening party, terrified. "It's all right," said Silky, stroking him. "We won't let them get you, Woffles. Don't be afraid."

Moon-Face and Jo went back to the others. "I
don't see what we can do," whispered Moon-Face.
"All the doors are locked, and we certainly can't
get keys to unlock them, for the one Brownie
Long-Beard had was the only one that could
unlock those cave-doors. And the Trolls are
guarding that rabbit-hole too well for us to get
down it. Even at night there will certainly be
someone there to guard it."

"Do you think perhaps we could get the rabbits
to tunnel silently somewhere else?" said Jo. "If
only they could make a way for us somewhere,
we could all pour in and surprise the Trolls."

"It's about the only thing to do," said

Moon-Face. "What do you think, Watzisname?"

"I think the same," said Watzisname. "If we can get the rabbits to make a really big hole, we might do something to surprise the Trolls. It's the only way we can get into the caves, isn't it?"

"Yes," said Moon-Face, thoughtfully. "Well, we'd better get to work at once. Where's Woffles?"

"Here, Mister Moon-Face!" said the rabbit eagerly. "Here I am. What am I to do? I daren't go down that hole I made, so don't ask me to!"

"I won't," said Moon-Face. "It was brave of you to go the first time. What I want you to do, Woffles, is to go and round up all the biggest and strongest rabbits in the Wood and get them here. Then we'll set them to work quickly on a burrow that must come up right in the very centre of the jewel-caves. Maybe the robbers won't expect us to force a way there. They will expect us to come through the walls, not under the floor of the caves."

"Right, Mister Moon-Face!" said the rabbit, and sped off, his white bob-tail jerking up and down as he went down the tunnel.

It was rather dull, waiting for the rabbits to come. The lantern nearby gave only a faint light. Moon-Face gave orders for everyone to speak in the lowest of whispers.

"I'm hungry!" whispered Connie.

Watzisname gave a little giggle. "I've got some Toffee-Shocks," he said. "Do you like sweets, Connie?"

"Oh *yes*," said Connie, pleased. "What's a

Toffee-Shock? I've never heard of one before."

Watzisname was holding out a paper-bag to Connie. The others watched. They knew Toffee-Shocks, which were very peculiar sweets. As soon as you began to suck a Toffee-Shock it grew bigger. It grew and it grew and it grew, till it completely filled your mouth and you couldn't say a word! Then, very suddenly, it burst into nothing, and your mouth was empty.

Connie took *two*! Gracious, what would happen? One was bad enough—but *two* Toffee-Shocks would fill her with astonishment and dismay!

She popped the sweets into her mouth. Everyone watched her. Bessie began to giggle.

Connie sucked hard. "It's funny," she thought. "The more I suck, the bigger they seem to be. Gracious, they were getting simply enormous!"

They were! They swelled up, as they always did, and filled Connie's mouth completely, so that she couldn't speak or chew! She stared at the others in horror.

"Gug-gug-gug," said Connie, in fright, her eyes almost falling out of her head. Her cheeks were puffed out with the swollen sweets, and her tongue was squashed at the bottom of her mouth.

Just as she thought she really couldn't bear it for one more moment, the Toffee-Shocks exploded, and went to nothing! Connie stood in the greatest amazement. Her mouth was empty. Where had the sweets gone? She hadn't swallowed them.

The others burst into giggles. Connie was really cross. "What a nasty trick to play on me!" she said to Watzisname, glaring at him.

"Well, you should only have taken one, not two," said Watzisname, wiping the tears of laughter from his eyes. "One Toffee-Shock is fun —but two must be awful!"

"Sh! Sh!" said Moon-Face. "Don't let the Trolls know we are still here. They will be on the watch if they think we are."

"Well, *I* think it would be a very good thing to stay here and make a noise," whispered Silky. "Then the Trolls will guard this hole, and keep their attention on us, which will give the rabbits a chance to burrow unheard."

"Silky's right," said Jo. "We'll talk loudly and make a noise. Then perhaps when the rabbits do their burrowing under the floor of the caves, the Trolls won't notice it."

So they all began to talk and laugh loudly. A third spear appeared at the entrance of the hole, and a voice said, "If you are thinking of getting down here, think again!"

"Your spears won't stop us when we charge down that hole!" yelled Moon-Face, which made a fourth spear appear, shining brightly.

In a little while a whole army of rabbits appeared at the back of the passage, jostling one another, headed by Woffles, who was bursting with pride again. "I've brought them," he said. "Here they all are, the biggest and strongest."

Moon-Face told them what he wanted them to do. "We want you to make a passage right *under* the caves," he said, "so that it comes up in the floor. The Trolls won't be expecting that. Whilst you're doing it. I'll send a message to the brownies in the Wood to come, and help us to burst through the tunnel you make, as soon as it is finished."

"The girls mustn't come into this," said Jo, as the rabbits began to burrow rapidly downwards. "They had better go back up the Tree with Silky. This may be dangerous."

"Oh, but we want to see what happens!" said Bessie, in dismay.

"We'll tell you what happens as soon as we know," promised Jo. "Silky, can you send a message to the brownies when you get above-ground?"

"I will," said Silky, and she and the three girls made their way back up the burrow and into the Wood. They met a brownie and gave him Moon-Face's message. He shot off at once to get a small army together.

The rabbits burrowed quickly and silently down into the earth, down and down and down. When they knew they were right underneath the centre of the jewel-caves, they began to burrow up again, up and up and up. They meant to come up just in the middle of the floor of the centre cave.

Brownies poured down into the tunnel. Everyone followed the rabbits closely, meaning to rush the caves as soon as the tunnel broke through the floor.

But alas! When the rabbits had burrowed upwards to the caves, they came to a stop.

Something hard and solid was above them. They couldn't burrow into it.

"What is it?" whispered Moon-Face, anxiously. "Let me feel." He felt. "It's heavy blocks of stone!" he groaned. "Of course, the floor of the caves is paved with stone. I had forgotten that. We can't possibly get through. I'm so sorry, rabbits —all your work has been for nothing!"

"Ha, ha, ho, ho!" suddenly came the distant sound of laughter. "*We* heard you burrowing! You didn't know the floors were made of stone! Ha ha, ho ho!"

"Horrid Trolls!" said Moon-Face, as they all made their way back down the tunnel. "Whatever can we do now?"

23. I

The Land of Know-Alls

"We'd better get back up the Tree, and tell Silky and the others we've failed," said Moon-Face, gloomily. "It looks to me as if the poor old Faraway Tree is done for. It's very, very sad."

They all went back up the Tree, and the brownies returned to their homes in the wood. Silky and the girls were very upset to hear that the rabbits hadn't been able to get through the floors of the caves.

"Heavy stone there," said Jo. "No one could burrow through that, or even move it. It's bad luck. There's no other way of getting down to the caves at all."

Everyone sat and thought. Nobody could think of any plan at all. "It isn't that we're stupid," said Moon-Face. "It's just that it's impossible."

"I suppose we couldn't ask anyone in the Land of Know-All for help, could we?" said Dame Washalot, at last.

"The Land of Know-All! Is that up at the top of the Tree now?" said Moon-Face, looking excited.

"Yes. Didn't you know?" said Dame Washalot. "I went up there this morning to find out how to do my washing in cold water, when I can't get enough hot. I found out all right, too. There's nothing they don't know up there!"

"Gracious! Perhaps they know how to get down into the caves then!" said Moon-Face. "Or maybe they could give us a key to open the doors."

"That wouldn't be much use," said Jo. "You may be sure the Trolls have put guards at the doors in case we thought of that. They are well-armed, too. It is only by taking them completely by surprise that we could defeat them."

"That's true," said Moon-Face. "Well, what about going up into the Land of Know-All? We might get some good advice. There are only five Know-Alls, and between them they know everything."

"Oh, do let's go now, this very minute!" said Connie, impatiently.

"All right, we will," said Jo, and he got up.

"I'll go and finish my washing," said Dame Washalot. "And hadn't you better see if your cakes are burning, Mrs. Saucepan? You left some in the oven."

"My goodness, so I did," said old Mrs. Saucepan, and climbed quickly down the tree.

The rest of them wanted to go into the Land of Know-All, even the Angry Pixie, who didn't often go into any of the strange Lands.

They all went up the topmost branch and climbed up the yellow ladder through the cloud. They came out into the Land of Know-All.

It was a small Land, so small that it looked as if anyone could fall off the edge quite easily here and there. In the very middle of it, on a steep hill, rose a magnificent glittering palace, with so many thousands of windows that it looked like one big shining diamond. From the middle of the palace rose a tremendously tall tower.

The children and the others went up two hundred steps to the great front door. Then they saw about a thousand servants lining the hall inside, all dressed in blue and silver. They all bowed to the little company at once, looking like a blue and silver cornfield blown by the wind, so gracefully did they bow at the same moment together.

"What is your wish?" said the thousand servants, sounding like the wind whispering.

"We want to see the Know-Alls," said Moon-Face, feeling rather awed.

"They are in the Tall Tower," said the servants,

and bowed again. Then a hundred of them took the little party to what looked like a small room, but which was really a lift. Ninety-nine servants bowed them in. One got in with them and pulled a silver rope. The children and the others gasped as the lift shot up the tower. It went so very fast. Up and up and up it went, till the children thought surely they would land on the moon!

At last the lift slowed down and stopped. The door slid open. The children saw that they had come to the top of the Tall Tower. It was surrounded on all sides by wide windows, and the children gasped with amazement as they looked out. Surely they could see the whole world from those windows! Oceans, seas, lands spread out on each side of them, and lay glittering in the brightest sunlight they had ever known.

Then they saw the five Know-Alls. They were strange, wonderful and peculiar folk, so old that they had forgotten their youth, so wise that they knew everything.

Only their calm, mysterious eyes moved in their old, old faces. One of them spoke, and his voice came from very far away—or so it seemed.

"You have come to ask for advice. You want to know how to get into the jewel-caves?"

"How does he know?" whispered Connie to Jo in amazement.

"Well—he's a Know-All," said Jo. "Sh! Don't talk now. Listen!"

Moon-Face knelt down before the wise Know-All, and spoke earnestly. "The Faraway Tree is

165

dying. It is because there are Trolls in the jewel-caves underground, cutting the roots that give the great Tree its life. How, oh great and wise Master, can we get down to the caves and stop them?"

The wise Know-All shut his gleaming, mysterious eyes as if he were thinking or remembering something. He opened them again and looked at Moon-Face.

"There is only one way. Your Slippery-Slip goes to the foot of the tree, down its centre. Bore down still farther, from your Slippery-Slip, and you will at last come out right under the Tree, in the centre of its tangled roots. Then you can surprise the Trolls and overcome them."

Everyone looked thrilled. Of course! If only they could make the Slippery-Slip go deeper down and down and down, they would come out in the middle of the roots! It was a marvellous idea.

"Thank you, oh great and wise Master," said Moon-Face, joyfully. "Thank you! We will go straight away and follow your advice!"

The little party bowed to the five strange Know-Alls, with their calm, mysterious eyes. Then they stepped into the lift, and the little servant pulled on the silver rope.

"Oh!" gasped everyone as the lift moved swiftly downwards. It really seemed as if it was falling! It slowed down at last, and the children and everyone else walked out into the vast hall.

Down the steps they went, and back to the hole in the cloud, feeling excited and a little queer.

The five Know-Alls always made people feel strange.

"Well," said Moon-Face, when they were safely in his curved room, and were beginning to feel a little more ordinary. "Well, now we know what to do. The next thing is—how do we bore a hole down through the rest of the Tree to its roots? I haven't any tools big enough to do that."

"You know," said Silky, suddenly, "you know, Moon-Face, there is a caterpillar belonging to a Goat-Moth, that bores tunnels in the trunks of trees. I know, because I've seen one. It had made quite a burrow in the wood of the tree, and it lived there by itself till it was time to come out and turn into a chrysalis. Then, of course, it changed into a big goat-moth."

"You don't surely think that a little caterpillar could burrow down this big Tree!" said Jo.

"Well, if Moon-Face could get about twelve of these goat-moth caterpillars, and could make them ever so much bigger, they could easily eat their way down, and make a way for us," said Silky.

Moon-Face slapped his knee hard and made everyone jump. "Silky's got the right idea!" he said. "That's just what we will do! We can easily make the caterpillars large. Then they can burrow down fast. Silky, you're really very clever."

Silky blushed. It wasn't often she had better ideas than Moon-Face, but this time she really had thought of something good.

"Now we'll have to find out where any goat-moth caterpillars are," said Moon-Face. "What tree do they usually burrow in, Silky?"

"There is one in the big elm-tree, and two or three in the willows by the stream, and some in the poplars at the other side of the wood," said Silky. "I'll go and get them, if you like. They smell a bit horrid, you know."

"Yes, like goats, don't they?" said Watzisname. "They're funny creatures. They live for three years in the trunks of trees, eating the wood! Funny taste, some creatures have. Go and get some, Silky. Take a box with you."

Silky sped off on her errand, taking a big box from Moon-Face's curved cupboard. Jo looked at the time.

"I really think we ought to go, Moon-Face," he said. "It's getting awfully late. I suppose Silky will bring back the caterpillars soon, and you'll change them to enormous ones and set them to work to-night? We'll come back to-morrow morning and see how you are getting on."

"I shall rub the caterpillars with growing-magic when Silky brings them," said Moon-Face, "but it will take them all night to grow to the right size. I shall probably set them to work after breakfast, Jo; so come then."

Jo and the girls slid down the Slippery-Slip, shot out of the trap-door and made their way home. They were tired, but very thrilled. How they hoped they could defeat those Trolls, and perhaps save the dear old Faraway Tree!

"We'll go back to-morrow, first thing after

breakfast," said Jo. "I expect old Moon-Face will have worked out some brilliant plan by then. I only hope we punish those bad Trolls properly. Fancy not caring if they killed the Faraway Tree or not!"

"I can hardly wait for to-morrow," sighed Connie. "I really don't think I can." But she had to, of course—and to-morrow came at last, as it always does. What was going to happen then?

24.

A Surprise For the Trolls

Next morning, immediately after an early breakfast, the four children set off to the Faraway Tree. They felt sad when they got near it and saw how much more withered the leaves were.

"It looks almost dead already," said Jo, dolefully. "I don't believe we can save it, even if we defeat the Trolls to-day."

They climbed up. Moon-Face and Silky were waiting for them in the curved room. With them, in the room, were some very peculiar-looking creatures—eleven goat-moth caterpillars.

They were great flesh-coloured caterpillars with black heads. A broad band of chocolate-brown ran down their long backs. They were really enormous, like long, fat snakes!

"Hallo!" said Moon-Face, beaming round. "The caterpillars are nearly ready. I rubbed them with the growing-magic last night, and they have grown steadily ever since. They are almost ready to go down the Slippery-Slip now and start eating the wood away at the bottom, to go right down into the roots of the tree."

The caterpillars didn't say a word. They just looked at the children with big solemn eyes, and twitched their many legs.

"I think they're ready," said Moon-Face. "Now, Jo, listen! The caterpillars are going to burrow a way for us right through the bottom part of the trunk of the Tree, into the heart of its roots. They are going to crawl out and frighten the Trolls, who will probably run away. Then our job is to rush after them and capture them. All the brownies are ready at the foot of the Tree. They are going to climb in through the trap-door, as soon as the caterpillars have gone down into the roots."

Everyone listened to this long speech, and thought the plan was excellent. Moon-Face gave a cushion to the biggest goat-moth caterpillar, who curled himself up on it solemnly. Then off it whizzed down to the foot of the tree, followed by all the others, one after another.

The children gave the caterpillars a little time to burrow, and then followed them down the Slippery-Slip. When they got to the trap-door they shot out and saw dozens of brownies waiting there. Moon-Face climbed back in through the trap-door and looked by the light of a lamp to see what had become of the caterpillars.

All he could see was a tunnel eaten out,

going down and down into the roots!

"They're going fast!" he said, looking out of the trap-door. "Out of sight already! My word, fancy being able to eat wood like that."

Soon Moon-Face reported that he thought they might all follow down the way the caterpillars had made. Their strong jaws made easy work of the wood of the Tree, and they were now almost at the bottom, among the roots. It was time to follow them up, and help to surprise the Trolls.

Everyone but the three girls and Silky crept down the hole. Sometimes it was as steep as the Slippery-Slip, and they slid. It was dark, but everyone was too excited to mind. The girls and Silky waited impatiently by the trap-door. The caterpillars came to the end of the enormous trunk, and found themselves in a tangle of great rope-like roots, going down and down. They crawled among them, with Moon-Face holding on to the tail-end of the last one, so as not to lose the way.

They came out into the very middle of the biggest cave. There was no one there, though the sound of distant hammering or digging could be heard.

"No Trolls to be seen!" whispered Moon-Face to the others. "Sh! I can hear some coming now!"

Moon-Face and the others slipped back into the tangle of roots, but the great snake-like caterpillars went crawling on. Just as they came to the entrance of the cave, two Trolls came in, almost falling over the caterpillars. They gave a yell.

"Oooh! Snakes! Run, run! Snakes!"

They ran off, screaming. The caterpillars solemnly followed, all eleven of them in a line. They met more Trolls, and every one of them ran away shrieking, for they were really afraid of snakes —and they certainly thought these enormous caterpillars were some dreadful kind of snake!

"After them!" cried Moon-Face, and waving a stout stick in the air he led the way into the jewel-caves. In one corner was a great pile of glittering jewels. The Trolls had plainly found a fortune down there!

The Trolls were shouting to one another. "The caves are full of snakes! Hide! Hide!"

The robbers crowded into a cave, put a great stone at the entrance, and pressed against it to prevent the caterpillars from entering. When Moon-Face came up, he lowered his big stick and grinned round at the others.

"Our work is easy! They've shut themselves in, and we can easily make them prisoners!"

"Who's there?" called a Troll, sharply, hearing Moon-Face's voice.

"The enemy!" said Moon-Face. "You are our prisoners. Come out now, and we will keep off the snakes. If you don't give yourselves up, we shall push away the stone and let the snakes in!"

Jo giggled. It was funny to think that anyone should be so afraid of caterpillars. The creatures were quite enjoying themselves, crawling round and about, getting in everyone's way.

"We'll come out," said the Trolls' leader, after

talking to his men. "But keep off those snakes!"

"Hold the caterpillars, you others," whispered Moon-Face. "Now, all together—heave away the stone!"

The Trolls came out, looking very scared. They were glad to see that the "snakes" were being held back by Jo and the others. The brownies at once surrounded them, and bound their hands behind their backs.

"We'll keep them in prison till next week, when the Land of Smack comes back again," said the head brownie with a grin. "Then we'll push them all up the ladder, and see that they don't come down. They can move off with the Land of Smack —it will do them good to live there for the rest of their lives!"

Moon-Face stayed down in the caves whilst the brownies found the key, unlocked the doors and marched out the frightened Trolls. They were strange-looking folk, with large heads, small bodies, and large limbs.

"Let's have a look round and see what damage has been done to the Tree," said Moon-Face. "Just look!—see how they've chopped that root in half—and cut this one—and spoilt that one. The poor Tree! No wonder it began to wither and die."

"What can we do for it?" said Jo, anxiously.

"Well, I've got some wonderful ointment," said Moon-Face. "I'm going to rub the damaged roots with it—you can all help—and we'll see if it does any good. It's very magic. I got it out of the Land of Medicines, years ago, and I've still got some left. I hope it's still got magic in it."

Moon-Face took a little blue pot out of his pocket and removed the lid. It was full of a strange green ointment.

"Better send up for the girls and let them help too," said Jo. But just at that moment the girls and Silky came rushing up, led by Woffles. The brownies had told them all that had happened, and they had come down in great delight.

"We're going to rub the damaged roots with magic ointment," said Moon-Face, and he held out the blue pot. "Dip your fingers in it, everyone, and hurry up. We can't afford to waste a single moment now, because the poor old Tree is almost dead!"

The children and the others kept dipping their fingers into the pot of ointment, which, in a most magical way, never seemed to get empty. Then, with the green ointment on their fingers, everyone rushed about to find damaged roots. They rubbed the ointment well into the roots, and came back for more.

"Well," said Moon-Face, after two hours' very hard work, "shall we take a rest, and pop up to see if the Tree is looking any better? I could do with a cup of cocoa or something. Let's go and see if old Mrs. Saucepan has got some buns and will make us something to drink."

So they walked up through the rabbit-burrows, and then climbed the Tree to Dame Washalot's. To their great disappointment all the leaves were still curled up and withered, and the

Faraway Tree looked just as dead as before.

"I suppose the magic ointment isn't any use now," said Silky, sadly. "Poor, poor Tree. Moon-Face, shall we have to leave it if it dies? Will it be chopped down?"

"Oh, don't talk about such horrid things," said Moon-Face.

Suddenly Jo gave a shout that made them all jump.

"Look! The leaves are uncurling! The Tree is looking better. It really is!"

It was quite true. One by one the withered leaves were straightening out, uncurling themselves, waving happily in the breeze once more. And then, oh joy, the Tree grew its fruits as usual!

Large and juicy oranges appeared on all the nearby branches, and shone golden in the sun. The children put out their hands and picked some. They had never tasted such lovely oranges in their life!

"There are some pineapples just above us, and some white currants just below!" said Connie, in surprise. "The Tree is doing well, isn't it? I've never seen such a lovely lot of fruit before!"

"The magic ointment has begun its work," said Silky, happily. "Now the Faraway Tree will be all right. Thank goodness we found out how to capture those horrid Trolls, and how to cure the poor old Tree!"

Everyone in the Tree rejoiced that day. The folk of the Enchanted Wood came up and down to pick the fruit. Woffles the rabbit came, his eyes shining with pleasure to think he had helped to save the Tree. He was dressed in the Red Squirrel's old jersey, and was very proud of it.

"He gave it to me as a reward," said Woffles, proudly. "Isn't it perfectly lovely?"

"Yes — and you look perfectly sweet!" said Silky. "Come and have some coffee, you funny little rabbit!"

25.

The Land of Treats

Everyone was very, very glad that the dear old Faraway Tree was all right again. It had been dreadful to think that it was dying, and might have to be chopped down. Now it seemed to be better than ever.

The children visited it every morning to pick the fruit to take home for their mother to make into pies and tarts. Everyone in the Tree was doing the same, and old Mrs. Saucepan made quite a lot of money by selling fruit tarts to the people who went up and down the Tree.

The bad Trolls, who had damaged the Tree's roots, had all been taken up to the Land of Smack, which was now at the top of the Tree.

"You should just hear the shouts and yells that those bad Trolls make up there," said Moon-Face with a grin, to the children. "They're having a dreadful time. They keep on trying to escape, and get down the ladder — but they can't."

"Why can't they?" asked Jo.

"Look and see," said Moon-Face, with a wider grin than before.

So Jo climbed up the topmost bough, and got on to the bottom rung of the ladder. He couldn't go any farther because on the other rungs were the goat-moth caterpillars, still simply enormous! There they were curled, like enormous snakes, waiting for the Trolls to try and escape.

"The Trolls are terribly scared of them," called up Moon-Face, "and as soon as they see them, they rush back into the Land of Smack. They don't know which is worse, snakes or smacks!"

The others giggled. "What are you going to do with the caterpillars when the Land of Smack has moved on?" asked Bessie.

"Oh, change them back to their right size again and take them to the trees we got them from," said Silky. "At present they are having pies and tarts to eat, instead of the wood they like—but we'd need to give them trees to gnaw if we fed them properly, they're big now! Still, they seem to like the pies."

"How long is this Land going to stay?" asked Connie, suddenly. "I hope it won't stay long, because I've got to go home soon. Mother's better and she's coming back, so I've got to go too. I don't want to, because it's such fun here."

"Well, you ought to be glad your mother is better and ready to have you home," said Jo. "You're a selfish little girl, Connie!"

"All the same, it *has* been such fun here," said

Connie. "You'd hate to leave the Enchanted Wood and the Faraway Tree and Moon-Face and Silky and the rest of your friends, you know you would!"

"Yes, we should," said Bessie. "Moon-Face, I wish a really nice Land could come before Connie goes—just for a treat for her, you know. Something like the Land of Birthdays, or the Land of Take-What-You-Please—or the Land of Goodies! That was lovely! Connie, some of the houses in the Land of Goodies were made of sweets and chocolate!"

"Oooh—how lovely!" said Connie. "Moon-Face, what Land is coming next?"

"Well—I rather think it's the Land of Treats, but I'm not quite sure," said Moon-Face. "I'll find out and let you know."

"The Land of Treats! What's that like?" said Connie, thinking that it sounded fine.

"Well—it's full of treats," said Moon-Face; "*you* know—donkey-rides, bran-tubs, Christmas Trees and ice-creams, and things like that."

"And circuses and pantomimes and clowns and balloons and crackers and . . ." went on Silky.

"Gracious!" said Connie, her eyes shining. "What a lovely Land that would be to visit for my last one. Oh, I *do* hope it comes before I go!"

It did! Two or three days after that, the red squirrel, dressed in his grand new jersey, arrived at the children's cottage with a message.

He rapped on the window, and made Mother jump. But when she saw it was the squirrel, she opened the window and let him in. She was getting quite used to the children's queer friends now.

"Jo! Bessie! Here's the red squirrel!" she called, and the children came running in.

"Good morning!" said the squirrel, politely "I've come with a message from Moon-Face, and

Moon-Face says that the Land of Treats will be at the top of the Tree to-morrow, and are you coming?"

"Of course!" cried the children, in delight. "Tell Moon-Face we'll be there."

"I will," said the squirrel and bounded off.

The next day the four children all went up the Tree in excitement. A rope had again been run down through the branches, for hundreds of the Wood-folk were going up to the Land of Treats. Whenever a really nice Land was at the top, the Tree had plenty of traffic up and down!

Moon-Face, Silky, Watzisname and Saucepan were waiting for them impatiently. "There are elephants," said Silky. "They give you rides. I'm going on an elephant."

"And you can go up in a balloon," said Moon-Face. "Can't you, Saucepan?"

"Moon? Go to the moon? Can you really?" said Saucepan, looking excited.

"UP IN A BALLOON!" yelled everyone, and Saucepan looked startled.

"All right, all right! No need to shout," he said. "Come on, let's go now. I want a Treat."

The old Saucepan Man led the way up the topmost branch. The others followed. Soon they all stood in the Land of Treats.

It looked simply lovely. Near them was a large-size roundabout, with animals to ride—but they were live animals! How exciting!

"Oh—let's go on the roundabout!" said Connie.

"No—let's get ice-creams first," said Jo. "*Look* at these! Did you ever see such beauties?"

The ice-cream man was standing with his little cart, handing out ice-creams for nothing. They were enormous, and you could have any flavour you liked.

"You've only got to say 'Chocolate!' or 'Lemon!' or 'Pineapple!' and the man just dips his hand in and brings you out the right kind," said Moon-Face, happily.

"He *can't* have got every flavour there," said Connie. "I shall ask for something he won't have and see what happens."

So when her turn came she said solemnly, "I want a sardine ice-cream, please."

And hey presto! The ice-cream man just as solemnly handed her out a large ice-cream, which was quite plainly made of sardines because the others could see a tail or two sticking out of it!

"Ha, ha, Connie! Serves you right!" said Jo.

Connie looked at the ice-cream and wrinkled up her nose. She handed it to the ice-cream man, and said, "I won't have this. I'll have a strawberry ice, please."

"Have to eat that one first, Miss," said the ice-cream man. So Connie had to go without her ice-cream, because she didn't like the taste of the sardine one, and couldn't eat it. She gave it to a cat who came wandering by looking for *his* Treat, which he hoped would be mice sandwiches.

"Now let's go on the roundabout," said Jo, when he had finished his ice-cream. "Come on! I'm going on that giraffe."

"I shall have a lion," said Moon-Face, bravely. "I'll have that one. It looks quite tame, and it has such a wonderful mane."

Connie didn't feel like a lion or a giraffe. She thought she would choose an animal who really would be tame. So she chose a nice tabby cat, who stood purring, waiting for someone to mount her.

"Take your seats, please!" called the roundabout man, a most amusing fellow who turned himself round and round and round all the time his roundabout was going, and only stopped when the roundabout stopped too.

Fanny chose a duck that had a lovely quack, and the softest back she had ever sat on! Bessie liked the look of a brown bear. Silky chose a hen and hoped it would lay her an egg as it went round and round. Saucepan chose a large-size mouse, and Watzisname took a dog that wagged its tail the whole time.

The roundabout music began to play. The roundabout moved on its way, round and round and round, going faster and faster. Saucepan made his mouse move over to Connie, meaning to ask her how she was enjoying such a treat.

But this was a great mistake, because Connie was riding a cat. The roundabout man always put the mouse on the opposite side to the cat — and now here was the mouse almost under the cat's nose!

The cat gave an excited mew when it smelt the mouse. It shot out its paw, and the mouse squealed in fright. It leapt right off the roundabout, and Saucepan almost fell off. He clung to the large mouse, all his pans rattling and clanging.

The cat rushed off the roundabout after the mouse. The roundabout man gave a yell and stopped the roundabout. The children leapt off and gazed in dismay at Connie and the cat chasing Saucepan and the mouse!

"Gracious! I hope the cat doesn't eat old Saucepan as well as the mouse!" groaned Moon-Face.

26.

Good-bye to the Faraway Tree

Everyone in the Land of Treats stood and watched Connie's cat chasing Saucepan's mouse. Round and round and in and out they went, knocking over stalls of fruit and upsetting all kinds of little Folk.

The mouse ran into a hole in the ground, and Saucepan fell off with a crash. He stood in front of the hole and clashed a kettle and saucepan together, frightening the cat, who stopped so suddenly that Connie shot over its head.

it with a large-sized saucepan when he did at last get out. The gull thought it was a hat and put it on proudly.

"Now, what next?" said Jo, when they had all had enough of the boats. "What about something to eat. There's an exciting place over there, where you can get anything you like, just by pressing a button. Let's try it, shall we?"

So they went to the curious little counter, behind which stood a smiling pixie. There were buttons all over the counter, which could be pressed. As you pressed them, you said what you wanted, and it at once came out of a little trap-door in the side of the counter.

"I'll have cold chicken, cold sausages, and salad," said Jo, who felt hungry. Moon-Face pressed a button for him, whilst Jo watched the trap-door. It opened, and out came a plate with chicken, sausage and salad on it. Jo took it in delight and went to sit at a nearby table, which was set with knives, forks and spoons.

"What will *you* have, Silky dear?" asked Saucepan, who was longing to press a button.

"Pear-tart," said Silky. "And cream."

Saucepan pressed a button and spoke loudly. "Bear-tart and cream!"

At once a tart shot out of the trap-door with a little jug of cream—but there were no pears in it—there were small teddy-bears, nicely cooked and arranged in rings in the tart.

"Oh Saucepan—I said *pear*-tart, not *bear*-tart!" said Silky, and she gave the plate back to the pixie behind the country. She pressed a button herself, and a delicious tart made with pears came out of the trap-door. Silky joined Jo at his table.

"I'll have a big chocolate pudding," said Moon-Face as he pressed a button, and out came the biggest chocolate pudding he had ever seen.

Saucepan pressed a button and got out a treacle pudding and cucumber sandwiches. He went off to a table by himself to eat them.

Everyone got what they wanted. In fact, they had more than they wanted, because it really was such fun to press the buttons and get something else. The buttons were marvellous and they produced anything that anyone asked for. Even when Connie asked for a ginger bun stuffed with carraway seeds, iced with chocolate, and scattered with small boiled sweets, the button she pressed made exactly what she wanted come out of the trap-door. Connie said the bun tasted really lovely.

They went over to the circus after that, and had a most exciting time, especially afterwards when anyone who liked could have a ride on the circus elephants. The elephants were very solemn and kind, and once when Connie wobbled a bit, one of the elephants lifted up his trunk and held her on.

Then they went into a magician's room and sat down in a ring on the floor to watch him do magic. He was the best conjurer anyone had ever seen.

"Ask me what you want, and I will do it!" he cried, after every trick, and then somebody or other would call out something very difficult. But, without any delay, the magician would do it.

"Make roses come in my kettle!" said Saucepan, suddenly, and he held out one of his kettles.

"Easy!" said the magician, and rapped on the kettle with his wand. Immediately a smell of roses came into the room. Saucepan took off the lid, and put in his hand. He pulled out dozens of deep-red, velvety roses. He gave one to everyone to wear.

"Make me fly round the room!" cried Connie, who had always longed to be able to fly. The magician tapped her shoulders, and two long blue wings shot out from them. Connie stood looking over her shoulder at them in delight.

Connie flapped them—and to her great joy she

flew into the air as easily as a butterfly, hovering here and there as light as a feather.

"Oh, oh! This is the greatest Treat I've ever had!" she cried, and flew round once again. Then, as she came to the ground, the magician tapped her once more and the wings disappeared. Connie was disappointed. She had hoped she would be able to keep them. She wouldn't have minded going back home a bit, if only she could have taken her wings with her.

The magician took a couple of goldfish out of Jo's ears. "What a place to keep goldfish, my boy!" he said. "You should keep them in a bowl of water."

"But—but," began Jo in surprise.

The magician took a bowl from the top of Silky's head, made Jo lean over sideways, and filled the bowl with water that seemed to come out of Jo's ear. It was really most extraordinary. He gave the goldfish to Jo.

"Now don't you keep those goldfish in your ears any more," he said. "You keep them in that bowl!"

Everyone laughed at Jo's astonished face.

"I'll take them home to Mother," he said. "She has always wanted goldfish."

Just then a bell rang loudly. "Oh! What a pity! It's time to go," said Moon-Face, getting up. "They turn you out of the Land of Treats every evening, you know. No one is allowed to stay for the night. It's too magic. Come on, we

Rather sadly they went to the hole in the clouds, with a crowd of other visitors. They went down to Moon-Face's, and there Connie said good-bye.

"I'm going home to-morrow," she said, "but I *have* had a wonderful time, really I have. Good-bye, Moon-Face, and thank you for rescuing me off the Ladder-That-Has-No-Top. Good-bye, Watzisname, I hope you remember your real name sometime. Good-bye, dear little Silky; it has been lovely to know you. Good-bye, Saucepan! I'm sorry you thought I was a horrid little girl."

Saucepan heard, for a wonder. "Oh, you're much nicer now," he said, "much, much nicer. Come back again. You may get nicer still then!"

They all went down the Tree. Connie said good-bye to the little red squirrel. "You're the best little squirrel I ever knew! Good-bye!" she said.

They went through the Enchanted Wood, and the trees whispered to Connie. "Wisha-wisha-wisha!"

"They're wishing me good-bye," said Connie. "Oh Jo, Bessie, Fanny—how lucky you are to live near the Enchanted Wood, and to be able to go up the Faraway Tree whenever you like. I wish I did too!"

So do I, don't you?

More Beaver Books

We hope you have enjoyed this Beaver Book. Here are some of the other titles:

The Adventures of Mr Pink-Whistle Mr Pink-Whistle is a funny little half-brownie man, and when he decides to help all the unlucky people in the world he has lots of amusing adventures! Written by Enid Blyton and illustrated by Rene Cloke; for younger readers

Mr Noah's Birthday All the people and animals on the Ark are celebrating Mr Noah's birthday with a grand birthday concert. But then Shem loses the music and this time even Crockle can't help – or can he? Written and drawn by John Ryan for younger readers

Play It Alone! A Beaver original. Over 150 fun ways of passing the time on your own, from solving puzzles and answering quizzes to playing yourself at ping-pong and volleyball. Written by Gyles Brandreth and illustrated by David Mostyn

These and many other Beavers are available from your local bookshop or newsagent, or can be ordered direct from: Hamlyn Paperback Cash Sales, PO Box 11, Falmouth, Cornwall TR10 9EN. Send a cheque or postal order made payable to the Hamlyn Publishing Group, for the price of the book plus postage at the following rates:
UK: 45p for the first book, 20p for the second book, and 14p for each additional book ordered to a maximum charge of £1.63;
BFPO and Eire: 45p for the first book, 20p for the second book, plus 14p per copy for the next 7 books and thereafter 8p per book;
OVERSEAS: 75p for the first book and 21p for each extra book.

New Beavers are published every month and if you would like the *Beaver Bulletin*, a newsletter which tells you about new books and gives a complete list of titles and prices, send a large stamped addressed envelope to:

Beaver Bulletin
The Hamlyn Group
Astronaut House
Feltham
Middlesex TW14 9AR